Off With their Heads

The Prequel to
Alice in Deadland

Mainak Dhar

TABLE OF CONTENTS

GREETINGS FROM THE DEADLAND

IN LATE NOVEMBER OF 2011, I uploaded my novel Alice in Deadland to the Kindle store using Amazon's KDP self-publishing program. I had first discovered the tremendous opportunity in reaching readers worldwide through the Kindle store in March, and after a modest beginning (I sold 118 ebooks in my first month), I was beginning to see some success, having sold some 20,000 ebooks by November. However, nothing had prepared me for the reception my story about a girl called Alice in a dystopian world called the Deadland got from readers. Alice in Deadland quickly became an Amazon.com bestseller and encouragement from readers like yourself led me to write the sequel, Through The Killing Glass, which was published in March 2012.

As of May 2012, the two Alice in Deadland novels had been downloaded by well over 100,000 readers on the Kindle store. This was the kind of reception most writers dream of, and certainly more than I had ever expected. I received more than two hundred reader emails and also started a Facebook group for Alice in Deadland fans (at http://www.facebook.com/groups/345795412099089/). The feedback I got was pretty unanimous—readers wanted to know more about the world that Alice found herself in. How had our civilization been reduced to the Deadland? What was the story behind some of the characters readers encountered such as the Queen and Bunny Ears?

That feedback motivated me to write this book. While Off With Their Heads is a prequel to the Alice in Deadland story, it serves a dual purpose. For readers who have already read one or both volumes in the series, this can serve as a great backgrounder on some of the pivotal characters in Alice in Deadland. Also, for readers who have never read one of my Alice in Deadland books, this can be a great starting point, setting the stage for the action that follows in those books.

Will there be more books in the Alice in Deadland series? It all depends on you, dear reader. As long as you keep reading, I'll keep writing.

Mainak Dhar

THE ACCIDENTAL QUEEN

'STAN, WHAT HAVE WE DONE?'

Dr. Protima Dasgupta was struggling to choke back her tears as she spoke to her colleague many thousands of miles away in the United States.

'Protima, I'm a bit busy. I'll talk to you later.'

Protima slammed her phone down. Even Stan, one of the most outspoken critics of the decision to use Sample Z in what the spooks had euphemistically called 'accelerated field tests', was no longer talking to her. She had spent more than twenty years of her life serving the United States Government, but it was as if her decision to leave the project and come back to India had burnt all bridges with friends and colleagues.

She walked unsteadily to the dining table and poured herself another glass of wine. She had been stupid to call Stan. It was likely his phone was tapped, but she was beyond caring now. She had argued that even if one disregarded the morality of using Sample Z on foreign populations, it was just too unstable to use yet. But of course, she had been overridden, and a week later, Global Hawk stealth drones had dropped canisters of the biological agent onto a Red Army garrison in Inner Mongolia.

Dr. Protima was not senior enough to be privy to the decision-making process, but she was senior enough to access some of the documents passed between her bosses and the men who had ordered the mission.

A shot across the bow to show them we still have an edge.

A reminder of who the superpower really is.

Those were two lines she remembered. Tensions between the US and China had reached a boiling point over the last year, with the US economy tottering and China reeling under increasing protests demanding democracy and human rights. The US had slammed the second Tiananmen Square massacre, only to be blamed by China for supporting what it called 'terrorist activity' in China to distract the US population from its economic woes. A humiliating bloody nose given to the US Navy off Taiwan had added injury to the considerable insult of the US economy having now been reduced to surviving on Chinese holding of its debt.

The fact that the garrison in Mongolia housed research facilities engaged in China's own biological warfare program was of scant consolation as Protima saw the chaos unfold on TV. When reports had come in of a strange virus spreading throughout Mongolia that turned people hyper-aggressive, attacking anyone in sight , she knew her worst fears had come true.

Sample Z had begun as a potential miracle cure for troops whose nervous systems had been badly damaged by battlefield injuries. Initial trials had been exciting, with troops doctors had given up on making recoveries to lead near-normal lives, and Protima had been exhilarated at being part of something that would help save thousands of lives. Then came the fateful meetings three years ago, when Protima and her team were asked to work on modifying Sample Z to incapacitate enemy troops, destroying their nervous systems and rendering them incapable of rational thought. A separate team had been working on another strain to dramatically enhance the strength and endurance of troops, turning them into berserkers immune to pain. Protima had warned that the differences between them were still not fully understood and the virus was very unstable. Ultimately, her objections had counted for little, and she had quit the program.

The scrolling news bar on the TV announced that there were at least ten thousand confirmed fatalities in China in the last week from the mysterious virus.

Protima turned off the TV and slept fitfully, dreaming of men with their faces peeling off, running towards her to attack her.

The next morning, she woke up to a beautiful summer morning, with the sun streaming through the windows of her hotel room. She pulled aside the curtains and saw the road already rapidly filling with the chaotic traffic that was the norm for New Delhi. She had a job interview at eleven o'clock, so she dressed quickly. She looked at herself in the mirror and for a moment she was looking at a stranger. Her grey hair was the same as usual, as were her lean, gaunt features. But her eyes, which normally sparkled with laughter, were now ringed with dark circles, and try as she might, she could not bring back the smile that had been a permanent feature on her face. After losing her husband in an accident several years ago, Protima had worked hard to recreate herself from the nervous wreck she had become, and she had almost succeeded, till the past few days.

But now she had another chance to start over. While some of her work, like Sample Z, would never be known outside a small group with the highest security clearances, she had been published widely in fields related to genetic engineering and had been given glowing references by her former bosses on the condition that she sign a very strict non-disclosure agreement. So she had no doubt she would get the job with a leading research institute using genetic engineering to improve crop yields to feed India's rural poor. Finally her experience and knowledge would be put to some good use.

She was in a taxi on her way to the interview when her phone rang. It was Stan.

'I should have left when you did. They're all dead. They're all dead.'

Protima sat up with a jolt. Stan was slurring, as if he had been drinking. 'Stan, calm down. What happened? Have you been drinking?'

'Lab 12 burned down a few hours ago. Most of the people there are dead, and the few that made it...'

Protima felt a chill going down her spine. Close friends of hers had worked at Lab 12, located just outside Washington, where Sample Z had finally been weaponized for use in China.

'I don't know if it was the Chinese retaliating for what we did or if our own government is covering its tracks...'

'Stan, stop! Please stop! We're on an open phone line.'

What Stan said next scared Protima more than she

had ever been in her life. 'It doesn't matter. Nothing matters any more. What the news is saying about the outbreak in China is not even close to how bad it is. I've seen what happened to the survivors of Lab 12. Protima, it's like nothing we imagined. The media is trying to keep it quiet under government orders, but when the news breaks, it'll be too late. You need to save yourself and get the truth out. I've sent a package for you with files from our project and the orders to use it in weaponized form. There are also papers about experiments on prisoners in Afghanistan. Go and meet Gladwell at the Embassy there in New Delhi. He's an old friend and a good man.'

'You're in Washington. Why don't you get it to someone there?'

'It's too late for me now. They caught me printing out the files and I just managed to get away. They're here now. Goodbye, Protima.'

With that, the phone went silent. Protima tried calling him back, but there was no answer.

While she was waiting to be called in for the interview, Protima wondered if she would be able to go through with it. After what she had heard from Stan, she found it hard to concentrate. Her hands seemed to be shaking uncontrollably, and her heart was pounding. However, once she sat before the interview panel, she managed to control her nerves and her interview went very smoothly, but all the while she thought of Stan's call. When she got back to her hotel room, she checked the TV and the Internet, but there was no mention of the fire Stan had talked about. He seemed like he had been drinking, and he would have been hit hard by the use of their research in the Mongolia operation. Finally, she decided to get some fresh air and walked outside, sitting at a coffee shop overlooking the busy street.

It was now six in the evening, and the Delhi summer heat had begun to dissipate. Protima sipped on her coffee, contemplating her future. At the age of forty-seven, it seemed too late to make a fresh beginning, but she was going to try. She had left India more than twenty-five years ago, on a scholarship to the US for her Masters, and her work there had earned her an internship in the Centers for Disease Control and Prevention, working on studying viral strains. She had excelled there, and one day had been approached for a full-time position in the government, working on classified biological programs. Now, she would try and put that behind her. She would get an apartment, buy a car, and start afresh with her new job.

Protima was jolted out of her thoughts by the man at the next table exclaiming to a girl, 'Oh my God! Have you seen this video? They're saying the dead are coming back to life!'

Some wiseass at another table mumbled something about how he always felt like a zombie on Monday mornings, but nobody laughed.

~ * * * ~

Within minutes, dozens gathered around the young man who had the YouTube video playing on his phone. Several others were now checking the video on their own phones, and Protima saw from their horrified faces that something was very wrong. She was about to ask one of them what the matter was when the owner of the cafe

6

shouted above the din.

'Folks, it's on CNN now. Just quiet down and let's see what they're saying.'

Protima edged towards the TV set up above the bar, and saw the familiar shape of the US Capitol Building in the background as the young news anchor adjusted her mike and looked at the camera. Protima had been in New York when 9-11 had happened, and she had seen how shaken the news anchors had been. This anchor had the same expression. Protima hushed two young girls next to her so she could hear what was being said.

'The Department of Homeland Security has said that it is premature to say whether the outbreak is a possible act of terror and has dismissed any link to the fire last night at a government lab featured in Wikileaks documents as a possible biological weapons research lab.'

The news cut to blurry mobile phone footage. The moment Protima saw the group of men, she knew something was wrong. They seemed to be shuffling more than walking, with their heads and hands bent at strange angles, and occasionally one would violently jerk his head. Protima had seen those symptoms before, as side effects of Sample Z.

Two police officers walked into the path of the men and fired. Protima heard gasps around her as two of the men fell to the ground, their bodies jerking as bullet after bullet tore into them.

'Why are they shooting? What the hell is happening?'

Protima ignored the cries from those around her as she tried to think what might have happened. Clearly Stan had been right and there had been a fire at the lab. It was possible the vials of Sample Z might have been compromised and some people might have been infected. But why on Earth were the cops shooting at them?

That was when something even stranger happened.

The two men who had been hit by dozens of bullets got up and the group rushed towards the policemen, who ran in panic. Then the footage stopped. The anchor was back and was reading from a sheet of paper in her hands.

'The Department of Homeland Security has decided to place some affected neighborhoods of Washington under immediate curfew. Anyone seen outside without prior authorization after noon tomorrow will be presumed to be infected. They are requesting all citizens to cooperate while the authorities contain this outbreak.'

The anchor put the sheet down, and looked at the camera. Protima could tell this part was not scripted. The young woman crossed herself and said, 'God help us all.'

Protima spent a tortured night, trying to come to grips with the role she and her colleagues had played in unleashing the outbreak now devastating Washington. She tried to tell herself she had just been doing her job, but how would that make her any different from an accessory to murder? She tried calling Stan again, but his phone was switched off.

That night, as she watched events unfold on TV and the Internet, she realized there was no containing the outbreak. Cases began to be reported across the United States, and the symptoms were terrifyingly the same. Reports had been leaked of how the first infected had seemed to be dead, and then got up and attacked anyone in sight, biting and clawing them to infect them as well. Police were still maintaining their position that rumors of the infected being impervious to gunshots were unfounded, but more videos had been posted online.

When Protima went down to the lobby of the hotel, it was crammed with tourists and visiting businessmen. With the outbreak now reported in Canada and the United Kingdom, people were beginning to panic and trying to catch the first flights home so they could be with their families.

The Concierge greeted her as she passed. 'Dr. Dasgupta, a courier landed for you yesterday.'

The package was marked as diplomatic mail. She smiled, remembering Stan joking that he could never get into too much trouble no matter how insubordinate he was because he had a brother in-law in the Foreign Service. Clearly, Stan had been able to call in one last favor before... Protima stopped herself. Despite all that had happened, there was no proof anything bad had happened to Stan.

She opened the package and found a simple note addressed to her. It was in Stan's handwriting.

Dear Protima, if you're reading this letter then it's already too late for me. Just pray they have beer in heaven, or hell, or wherever people like me go.

When the pressure to weaponize Sample Z began, I got curious about what was going on. The upside is that I got my hands on these files, but the downside is that it's a matter of time before they get me. I don't know who to trust anymore. That's the reason I'm sending these to you instead of trying to get them to anyone in the government.

I don't know if we can stop what is happening—it may be too late for that. But at least people will one day know the truth behind how we ruined our world.

Do as you see fit. You could try sharing it with the press, but I don't know how free our free press is any more. The people I reached out to didn't want to have anything to do with this. But do get it to Gladwell at the American Embassy. He's a good man, and he is very well-connected. He could at least help us get this to someone in the government who is not in on the conspiracy. This is all part of a plan, but I fear the men behind this don't fully understand what they are unleashing.

Take care, my friend.

Protima put the note aside and took a look at the documents, wondering how much of what Stan had written was true. As she read the first page, she grabbed the sofa behind her for support and sat down. She read non-stop for over an hour, reading each document more than once to make sure she was not mistaken about their contents.

As much as she would have liked to not believe them, the documents were devastatingly clear. There were transcripts of conversations, emails, and minutes of meetings.

What Protima, Stan and their colleagues had been working on had been a very small part of a grand plan that was both awe-inspiring and terrifying in equal measure. Vials of Sample Z had been taken to remote bases in Afghanistan for human testing. The men who had ordered the use of Sample Z in China had known its likely effects much better than Protima had realized. But in keeping the scientists out of the loop, it seemed they had totally underestimated how the virus would behave once it was transmitted from one person to another.

Protima closed her eyes, her head throbbing. Could men really condemn millions to death for a plan that called for gradual repopulation to deal with the issue of scarce oil and other resources? Could the same men seek to quell rising discontent about the ruin the financial elite had brought to the West by creating such an environment of fear that people would gladly accept any form of tyranny? Was it possible that they had managed to forge some sort of partnership with sections of the Chinese government who were struggling to contain their own people's calls for democracy? The documents in front of Protima made it amply clear that was exactly what had happened.

The final contents of the package were two small vials containing a red liquid. Protima knew what they were. The vaccines they had been working on to protect against Sample Z. They were untested, but in sending them, Stan had at least given her a shot at life.

A commotion started around her. Several men and women were standing, pointing at a TV in the corner of the lobby. The first case of the outbreak had been reported in India. With millions of people traveling by air every day, and many in the neighborhoods surrounding Lab 12 not even aware of the risks, there was no telling how far and how fast the outbreak would spread.

Now that the outbreak had begun to spread globally, Protima knew she had very little time. She dialed the American Embassy to get an appointment with Gladwell.

~ * * * ~

'They say the disease makes people into demons who cannot be killed. My cousin saw a man at the airport who bit a dozen others and the police kept shooting him but couldn't put him down. You're lucky that your destination is on the way to my home. You are my last passenger for now. After I drop you, I'm going straight there and staying put with my family till they figure this out.'

The last thing Protima needed was a talkative taxi driver. Protima just nodded, but that seemed to encourage the man.

'I gave a lift to two Army officers, and they told me they were being called up for duty. But they also said they were getting contradictory orders. Nobody in the government has any idea what to do.'

Protima didn't envy anyone who was trying to deal with the unfolding situation. Any outbreak of a highly contagious disease, let alone one with such unpredictable and terrifying effects, was best nipped in the bud. Identify the core outbreak, quarantine those infected and contain the spread till the strain was better understood. In this case, it was way too late for that. The infection had spread globally, and after what Protima had just read, it was a fair bet some elements in the government had actively aided in its spread.

As she looked out the windows, the streets of Delhi were packed with policemen. But she shook her head as she saw that they had come prepared for riot control, with batons and shields. If the outbreak spread here, they would be of little use.

As the taxi turned towards the American Embassy, the taxi driver shouted, 'There's no way they will let me get any closer. You'll have to walk from here.'

Roadblocks manned by Indian policemen barred their entry to the approach road. Protima saw that the Marines who guarded the Embassy were now gathered at the gate, all armed with automatic rifles, and she saw movement on the roof, which could have been snipers. Clearly they were not taking any chances. As she tried to go towards the Embassy building, one of the policemen stopped her.

'This area is now closed to the public.'

Protima pleaded that she had an appointment at the Embassy but that did not seem to have any impact. Finally, she took out her American passport. 'Look at this, please. I am of Indian origin but hold an American passport. You cannot stop me from going to the US Embassy.'

The policeman looked like he was in doubt, but he was saved from having to make a decision by one of the Marines jogging over from the Embassy gates. 'Ma'am, please come with me.'

He jogged back without waiting for Protima and she walked as fast as she could. Closer to the Embassy, she saw the same emotion she had seen in the policeman's eyes. Fear.

The Marines might have looked intimidating from afar, with their weapons and body armor, but up close, most of them were very young, and they looked terrified. She was ushered into the main building, where she walked up to the receptionist.

'Excuse me, I have an appointment with the Chief of Mission, Robert Gladwell.'

The receptionist asked Protima to wait while she

called Gladwell's office. Protima sat down in the lobby, which was packed with US citizens who had come to the Embassy to seek refuge and try and get home. A woman was sobbing, her head buried in her husband's chest as he tried to comfort her. Protima caught only a few snatches of their conversation before they passed her. 'Martha, all flights are cancelled. We can't get out for now. The kids will be okay...'

The TV was playing CNN. The footage showed burning buildings somewhere and Protima walked closer to hear what was being said.

'Chinese and US naval forces have skirmished off the coast of Taiwan on the same day Israel claimed to have shot down two Iranian missiles. The President has ordered all US forces to be ready to deal with the unfolding crisis, and the Department of Homeland Security has reinstated the color-coding for the threat level to the US Mainland, declaring it to be red. In a separate announcement, the Department of Homeland Security has declared that many internal security duties are to be handed to the private military contractor firm Zeus, as US military forces were needed to deal with the multiple international crises that threaten to escalate to all-out war in Asia and the Middle East. One of the first actions of Zeus has been to forcibly disband all Occupy protests, saying that they suck up precious resources needed to control the outbreak and also that crowds spread the outbreak. Many civil rights activists protested, saying private armies cannot be used to silence US citizens' fundamental rights to free speech and assembly. The spread of the outbreak continues unabated, and the Center for Disease Control has said it will stop issuing casualty figures as they are growing at such an exponential rate.'

Protima sat down, her hands shaking as they gripped the package. The plans outlined in the documents Stan had sent her were unfolding right before her eyes.

Someone coughed to get her attention and she looked up to see the receptionist. She was an aging Indian woman who had dark circles under her eyes and looked dog-tired.

'Dr. Dasgupta, I'm afraid Mr. Gladwell is unable to meet you now. As you know, things are busy here and he has some urgent matters to attend to.'

Protima felt her heart sink. 'I had an appointment with him. I just need to meet him for a couple of minutes.'

The receptionist was polite but Protima sensed she was being evasive. 'I'm sorry, but he himself has asked me to cancel this meeting. I can't help you.'

There was no way she was going away without giving the documents to Gladwell. Protima tried again, pleading with the receptionist. 'Please, please give me just two minutes with him. I don't even need to talk to him. I just need to give him some very important documents.'

'Dr. Dasgupta, I presume. Chief Gladwell asked me to apologize for not being able to meet you, but if I can help you in any way, please let me know.'

Protima turned towards the deep, gravely voice to find herself looking up at a tall, bald man built like a tank who completely dwarfed her. He was wearing a military uniform and even indoors his eyes were covered by wraparound sunglasses.

'Ma'am, my name is Major John Appleseed, and I can pass on whatever you wanted to give to Bob.'

With the unthinking trust most people had for men in uniform, Protima held out the parcel, but as he grabbed it, she paused. Stan had told her to give the package only to Gladwell. She started to retract her hand, but Appleseed held on. There was still a smile on his lips, but his voice had a hard edge to it now.

'I said I will take it from here.'

Their impasse was broken when somebody shouted and Protima turned to look at the TV. A news channel was broadcasting live from the gardens surrounding India Gate, in the very heart of Delhi. There was the sound of gunfire and of people screaming and as the cameraman zoomed in, Protima saw a group of men walking in a shuffling gait, many of them covered in blood. The camera zoomed in again and she saw that one of them had half his face torn off. More people in the reception screamed, and someone bumped into Appleseed, throwing him off balance for a second. Before he could recover, Protima was running out the door, heading into a city that, like many others around the world, was now faced with its worst nightmare—a highly contagious, deadly virus that turned people into raging monsters.

~ * * * ~

Protima managed to get a cab that took her halfway to her hotel, but the driver refused to go any further, saying it was too dangerous. Protima tried hailing other cabs, but nobody stopped. As she walked along the road, she saw that the policemen outside had disappeared. Some small shops across the street were being looted and an old man was lying on the ground. There seemed to be no law and order in sight, and she realized that she was alone and defenseless in the middle of a city that had given into terror and anarchy.

A commotion began further down the street and a man staggered onto the street. His clothes were torn and he was bleeding from a gash on his neck. He cried out to her for help but before she could cross the street, he fell to the ground. A woman emerged from the bushes behind him. She was covered in blood, with the shuffling gait of the infected, and her eyes were vacant and yellow. She shrieked as she saw Protima and began to cross the road to reach her. The wounded man, whom Protima had assumed to be dead, sat up and turned towards her. His eyes had a similar blank expression and he too screamed and got up to chase Protima.

Protima was now running as fast as she could, her heart hammering. She stumbled and fell, scraping her right knee on the pavement. She turned to see the bloodied couple still following her, and she scrambled to her feet, ignoring the pain in her knee as she started running again. After a few minutes, she stopped to catch her breath, and saw that the couple were now far behind. Protima bent over, her breath coming in jagged gasps, thankful that the infected did not seem to move very fast. Protima saw an abandoned bicycle and began pedaling it, hoping that getting back to the hotel would mean at least some period of safety for her to consider what to do next.

As she rode, she saw all around her the signs of a city that was tearing itself apart. Several pillars of smoke rose above the city's skyline and people were running all around, and every now and then she got terrifying glimpses of groups of the infected, hunting people down like packs of wild animals. There were no policemen or troops in sight, though Protima wondered what good they would have been against an enemy that could not be killed.

She finally met a small group of policemen huddled near a shop. The officer had a pistol in his hand, and the four constables with him were carrying rifles. The officer waved her down.

'Miss, you can't go that way, the entire neighborhood is crawling with Biters.'

'I need to get to the Taj Hotel.'

The officer shook his head sadly. 'Miss, from what I hear, there are Biters running wild around there. Why don't you go home?'

There was no longer any home for her. Protima got on the bike and rode in a different direction, no longer sure of what she would do or where she would go. When she had learned of the plan outlined in Stan's documents, she had agreed with his assessment that the men who had planned this were playing with fire. But now having seen firsthand what the infection did to people, she feared there was no real way to contain it. Like a wildfire, it would consume everything in its path before it burned itself out.

She had been so lost in her thoughts that she almost did not notice the black SUV just a few meters behind her and closing fast. It careen towards her and she swerved out of the way just before it could hit her bike. The front windows were down, and she could see the driver and one more man. Both were Caucasian, wearing dark suits and wraparound sunglasses. She had seen many men like them during her time in Washington. Government agents.

At first, she thought nearly knocking her down was an accident but then the driver leaned out. In his hand was a pistol. Protima was so startled that she lost her balance and the bike hit a bump on the sidewalk, sending her sprawling to the ground. That saved her life as the man fired and the bullet slammed into the wall over Protima's head. The man was shouting something, but Protima's ears were still ringing from the gunshot and she could not fully understand what he was saying.

Protima sat against the wall, shocked. No US government agents would be openly shooting at someone in the streets of Delhi.

The driver stopped the SUV and got out, walking towards her, the gun pointed at her. The second man remained in the car, but he now had a gun pointed at her as well. The man stood over her and said, 'Dr. Protima, I believe you have a package for us.'

Realization dawned on Protima as she recalled the confrontation she had with Appleseed back at the embassy. She stood up gingerly, feeling her ankle. The man's expression was inscrutable behind his dark glasses.

'Who are you? What right do you have to attack an American citizen?'

The man smiled. 'Look, Doctor, I don't want this to be any more difficult than it has to be. You're in way over your head here and you have no idea about just how far my bosses can go to get the material you have in your hands. Just give me the damn package and you won't hear from us again.'

It would be tempting to hand over the package, but could she live with the knowledge that she had done nothing? Tens of thousands had already died, and God alone knew how many more would die before it was all over. Her heart pounding, she took a step back. 'Young man, I have no doubt you could take this from me, but I will not hand it to you.'

The next thing Protima knew, she was on the ground, her head splitting with pain and warm blood flowing down the side of her face. The man raised his gun again.

'Look, lady, I don't take any pleasure in hitting old women, but I do need to do this.'

He leaned down to grab the package from Protima's hand. That was when his partner screamed from inside the SUV.

'Greg, they're coming. Hurry up!'

~ * * * ~

Protima looked beyond the man in front of her to see a crowd of at least twenty of the infected converging on the car. A couple of men in bloodied and tattered suits were mixed up with men and women wearing the rags of slum dwellers. They all had that vacant expression and many of them had blood from other victims running down the sides of their mouths. The man inside the car fired again and again, and three or four men went down, only to get back up within seconds. The man inside the car was screaming as he was pulled out and the crowd tore into him, clawing at him and biting into his face.

'Goddamn Biters!' the man in front of Protima growled. He shouted into his earpiece. 'We're under attack by Biters. Are there any other Zeus units nearby who could help?'

Zeus. Protima had heard that name before somewhere, but she had no time to think as some of the infected now came around the car towards her. The man in front of her pointed his gun at the approaching crowd, shooting several times till his magazine emptied. All he did was enrage them further, and they began to emit a high-pitched screech as they surrounded him. Protima took advantage of the situation to get back on her bike, and she pedaled away, forcing herself not to look back even when she heard the man's screams and cries for mercy.

Now all around her she saw signs of the infection spreading. There were several dead bodies littering the street, and two of the infected wrestled down and killed a large man who had tried to fight back. She realized that while they first tried to infect others by biting them, any significant resistance led them to kill their prey.

Tears were freely streaming down Protima's face as the world fell apart. When people at the highest levels of government had brought about such a catastrophe, what hope did a frail old woman like her have of fighting back?

Two more of the infected crossed her path, and she turned her bicycle sharply to the right to avoid them. Biters. That was what the man who had attacked her had called them. She wondered, as the infection spread around the world and more and more people fell to it, would people give it a name? Some terrible infections in the past had been trivialized by the names they had been given—bird flu, swine flu. What would this scourge be called? Would there even be enough people left to give it a name?

Now, further away from the open spaces around the Embassy, she had entered a congested market. Khan Market, if her memory served. The closely packed shops and cars parked in front of them had made it a deathtrap. Hundreds of Biters milled around and a few corpses lay around the front of the shops. A small group of policemen had tried to make a stand and Protima almost gagged at what remained of them—little more than the bloody shreds of their khaki uniforms.

The front wheel of her bicycle caught on something and her bike buckled under her. She was thrown forward, landing hard on the ground. The wind knocked out of her, Protima scrambled to get up, but slipped and fell again. She had attracted the attention of a few Biters and they were converging on her. She felt around and found a rock the size of her fist. The nearest Biter was now no more than a dozen feet away, a thin man with half his face ripped off wearing a bloodied and torn suit. Protima threw the rock as hard as she could, and it hit the Biter squarely on the head. He staggered back, but then he looked at her with vacant, red eyes and screamed, blood tricking down the sides of his mouth. Four others joined him and they came towards Protima.

Protima tried to scream for help, but not a sound came out. She tried to get back on her feet but a cold, clammy hand grabbed her leg. Suddenly, someone else grabbed her and yanked her back. Protima pulled away, but whoever was holding her was too strong. She found herself looking into the face of a young man wearing large rabbit ears on top of his head.

'Come on!'

He pulled her behind him on his bike and as the Biters roared in anger, he rode away at high speed.

For several seconds, Protima did not say anything. Instead she just clutched her unlikely savior, thankful for her narrow escape. Finally, the man spoke.

'Look, I need to get to my girlfriend's place. Where can I drop you?'

Protima's mind was a blank. Where could she go that was safe? Was anywhere safe any more?

The man spoke, a tinge of irritation in his voice. 'You must have a home or a family somewhere?'

Protima started to say something but all that came out was a stifled sob. The man stopped the bike and turned to look at her, his voice considerably softer.

'I'm sorry. Things are crazy and I just want to make sure she's okay. I'll drop you wherever you want, just tell me where.'

Protima got her first good look at him and realized that he was very young, perhaps a college student, with kind eyes.

'Young man, you have done quite enough for me. Just drop me ahead near the India International Center. It doesn't yet look overrun and I can see a lot of policemen in front of it.'

He took her near the gate and as she dismounted, he smiled.

'There must be something really important in that packet you're carrying. You didn't let go.'

Protima looked at the bundle of documents she was carrying. Having failed to give them to Gladwell, did they really matter any more? Given how deep the conspiracy ran, would it have mattered even if she had been able to meet him? She wished the man luck as he rode away.

A dozen police constables stood in front of the India International Center. Normally the venue of high-profile conferences and meetings, it was more than likely that there were high-level government officials or diplomats stranded inside. That would certainly explain the security, though Protima doubted the policemen would be much use. Several of them were huddled around a radio, and they looked terrified.

One of them saw her approach and beckoned her. 'Come inside, but I doubt any place is safe now. Not after what's happening around the world.'

Protima thought he meant the spread of the infection and she told him of what she had seen in the city. When she mentioned that the Biters seemed to be killing those who tried to resist being converted, she saw more than one of the policemen visibly blanch. The one who had spoken to her pointed to the radio and said, 'It's not just the bloody monsters, the whole world seems to have lost its mind.'

'What do you mean?'

When Protima asked him what he meant, he answered, a haunted expression in his eyes.

'Some elements in the Pakistani army launched nuclear missiles against our forward areas. It seems that Iran also launched missiles at Israel. It's not clear what exactly is going on but I think a nuclear war is either breaking out, or is taking place as we speak.'

Protima stood, chilled by what she had heard. The conspiracy behind the spread of the infection was one thing. Did laying waste to large parts of the world through nuclear exchanges also figure as part of the 'depopulation' plan? And if it did, what hope was left at all for anyone?

~ * * * ~

Protima walked into the complex. People wandered around as if dazed. There were a few foreign diplomats, several people who had gathered for a book discussion and many members who had come with their families for lunch. Now they were trapped in a city that was fast becoming a slaughterhouse. Some people huddled around a TV in the library. The news was on, and the anchor was facing the camera and reading from a prepared script. All pretense of normality had been discarded—her clothes were crumpled, she wore no makeup, and the dark circles under her eyes were obvious. As someone off-camera prompted her, she began reading.

'The infection is continuing to spread, and many cities are now totally cut off from all communication with the outside world. After the nuclear strike on Tel Aviv and retaliatory strikes on Tehran, the Middle East is in the grip of an all-out war. The Chinese government has for the first time publicly accused the United States of being behind this crisis by using illegal biological agents, a charge the US has denied. Tensions in the waters of Taiwan are high after two Chinese planes were shot down after approaching a US carrier. Closer to home...'

The woman paused and looked up at the camera, her eyes betraying just how horrified she was at the news she had been handed.

'Closer to home, rogue elements in the Pakistani military took advantage of the chaos to launch tactical nuclear weapons at two forward operating bases of the Indian Army. The Prime Minister has condemned the action and said that India will react with appropriate measures.'

Protima sat down against the wall, and while close to a hundred people were packed into the library, not a single word was said. What was there to say? Every single one of them was thinking the same thing Protima was—there was no longer any hope. It was only a matter of time before either the Biters got them or the unfolding nuclear madness claimed them.

Someone got up to turn off the TV, but several others pleaded with him to keep it on. A compromise was reached, and while the TV was kept on, it was put on mute. Protima kept staring at the screen, hypnotized. The worst nightmares of the human race were coming true, with visuals of nuclear mushroom clouds interspersed with the now-familiar images of marauding packs of Biters ravaging entire cities.

She was shaken out of her stupor by a man shouting at the top of his voice outside the library. A Caucasian man, his face reddening, shouted to no one in particular.

'I am the bloody Defense Attaché of the United Kingdom. I cannot be holed up here like an animal. Someone get on the phone to the bloody High Commission and tell them to get me out!'

Nobody stirred, and a woman tried to pacify him as his shouting gave way to sobs and he collapsed. It would take time to sink in that ranks and badges of status no longer counted for much.

A helicopter passed overhead and several people got up, shouting excitedly, pointing out the window.

'They've come to get us out!'

'Finally, we're saved!'

Protima looked out the window, and her heart sank. It was a small, black helicopter, certainly not one that could carry more than a couple of passengers. A single man stepped out, wearing black sunglasses and a dark suit. The British Attaché had raced out of the building and met the man as he approached the library. Protima strained to hear their exchange.

'Thank God you're here. Get me out. I'm the British Defense Attaché.'

The man who had just arrived fished into his pocket to take out a photograph, which he showed to the British diplomat.

'Have you seen this woman? Our aerial team saw her headed here.'

Protima felt her mouth go dry as she saw that the photograph was hers.

Getting no answer, the man pushed the diplomat out the way and walked towards the library. The British diplomat took the man by his shoulder, spinning him around.

'How dare you push me? Which government do you represent?'

The man calmly reached into his suit, took out a pistol and shot the diplomat in the head. Then he continued walking towards the library. Several people had witnessed the scene and screams rang out all around Protima as people scrambled towards the back of the library. The door swung open and the man walked inside. His eyes locked on Protima and he smiled.

'Doctor, I had hoped to meet you here. Now, will you

be kind enough to hand me the package or should I take it from you?'

There was a sudden barrage of firing outside and the man turned to see what was going on. That gave Protima the time to run deeper into the library. Hiding behind a bookshelf, she saw the man talk into his earpiece.

'She's here, but looks like the Biters are at the gate. I'll get the package and be out in a minute. Bloody Biters are everywhere.'

There was another rattle of gunfire and then it stopped. Protima thought of the policemen at the gate, but for now her greater concern was survival. She went deeper into the library, people screaming and sobbing all around her. The man pursuing her was now just feet away and through the gaps between the books, Protima saw the library door open once more. She caught a glimpse of khaki police uniforms and was about to call out for help when she stopped. The ones who had just entered the library were no longer policemen,. They had blood all over their tattered uniforms, and they shuffled inside the library, emitting low-pitched moans.

The Zeus agent turned and fired at the approaching Biters, and a couple of them went down. But there were too many of them entering the library and the people inside were screaming in panic, producing an ear-splitting crescendo. Protima didn't wait to see what happened. She ran further towards the back of the library. That was when she saw the vent. She pulled it open, breaking a couple of her nails in the process, and scrambled inside, crawling on all fours. From behind her came screams and the sickening sounds of teeth tearing into human flesh. Protima kept crawling and turned a corner, finding herself in total darkness. She clutched the package tighter, and moved forward, trying to feel ahead of her with her free hand. The floor moved under her hand and she tried to put more pressure on it to see how stable it was. The next thing she knew, a whole section of the piping gave way and she fell. She hit her head on something, and then there was darkness.

~ * * * ~

Protima woke up face down in something wet, her head aching terribly. She was lying in a pool of her own blood. As she tried to get her bearings, she realized she was lying in near-total darkness with a foul stench all around her. She felt a stab of panic as she tried to remember what had happened to the package she had been carrying. She felt around her for the envelope and clutched it to her chest as she sat up. Protima reached into her pocket to take out her mobile phone. As she shone it around her, she saw that she was inside drainage pipes or perhaps sewers. She had lost all track of time in her flight from the Biters, but with the mobile showing that it was now past seven in the evening, she must have been out for several hours. She drifted in and out of consciousness for some time before she finally managed to get herself up and walk down the tunnel.

Holding the mobile in front of her like a torch, she proceeded down the tunnel. She tried to brush away the wetness around her eyes, and when she saw the red smear on her hand, Protima gasped. She had no idea how badly she had been hurt, but there was no way for her to stop and check. She had to get to... safety. She stopped herself at that thought. There was no safety for her. If the Biters did not get her, the Zeus agents would.

She sat down against the wall, trying to collect her thoughts. Her stomach was rumbling, but hunger was the least of her worries. She had to push on and hope she could find a way up to the surface soon. What she would do then she forced herself not to think about.

Something brushed past her leg and she screamed, only to realize it had been a rat. When man had finished destroying civilization, perhaps rats would reclaim what remained. She got up and walked on, flashing her mobile in front of her every once in a while. It was now past two in the morning according to the display on her phone, but down here time did not matter. It was dark, with the floor covered in slime and puddles of water. Finally, unable to walk any more, Protima curled up against a wall and slept.

When she woke up, for a minute she hoped it had all been a nightmare and perhaps she was back in her hotel room. However, the musty odor and her dark surroundings told her that her nightmare was only too real. She walked some more, but realized that unless she ate or drank something, she would not last long. Water was more important to keep herself hydrated, so she forced herself to take a drink from a puddle of water. It smelt terrible and had a metallic tinge to it, but she forced it down.

Her fear and disorientation had given way to anger. Anger at the men who had brought so much destruction upon her and millions of others. No matter what it took, she would survive and get the truth out. She pushed on and smiled for the first time in many days as she saw a flicker of light up ahead. She could not tell how far it was, but at least there was hope. Her stomach continued to growl and she felt faint with exhaustion and hunger, but she kept going.

When she came closer to the light, she screamed in frustration. The beacon of hope she had been following was a single hole about a few inches in diameter in the roof through which daylight was streaming in. Protima sat down against the wall, drained of energy and hope. She tried to get back up but her legs did not have the strength. Through the light streaming into the tunnel, she took a look around and saw what appeared to be grass or leaves lying near her feet. The wind must have carried them through the hole in the roof. She picked them up, trying to determine if they were edible. Having already drunk the filthy gutter water, Protima was beyond the point where taste mattered, but she didn't want to eat something that could make her sick or worse.

She smiled a bit as the smell brought back long-lost memories of joints smoked surreptitiously in college. Ganja leaves were abundant in this part of India, and while they could not sustain her for long, it was better than dying of hunger. She bit down on the leaves and ate about half of them within seconds, tucking the rest into her pockets for later. A short nap later, she resumed her journey.

After a few more hours of walking, she began to feel giddy. Whether it was exhaustion or the ganja, she did not know, but she held onto the wall for support. Protima saw shadows ahead of her and called out, but there was nobody else there. She heard her husband call out to her, which was impossible. She stopped again, her head spinning, and sat down and took a nap before continuing.

As much as she knew it was messing with her head, hunger and desperation won over rational thought and Protima finished the rest of the ganja leaves over the next two meals. She thought she had been down for more than three or four days, but it was impossible to tell. More than once she saw light up ahead, only to find nothing more than small holes. She wondered what the world up there was like, whether there were any more people left, or if the whole world had now been infested with Biters. She wondered what the men who had brought this upon the world were doing now.

She sat down once again, trying to clear her head. She had found more ganja leaves, and they had left her in a dreamlike state. She knew she was hallucinating when she saw her husband, but it was beginning to feel good. She welcomed the thought that she was not alone down here. So when she heard her husband's voice, she would answer back.

That was when she heard the shuffling noises up ahead. Her mind snapped, as if waking from a dream. This was no ganja-induced hallucination.

She was not alone.

By now her eyes had begun to adjust to the dark and she saw a flicker of movement ahead of her where the tunnel curved to the left. She took out her mobile phone and held it in front of her, but its feeble light did little to illuminate whoever was coming her way.

'Hello, who's there?'

Protima regretted the words the moment they left her mouth for her question was answered by a series of grunts and screeches. Down here, in the dark and in the endless tunnels, there was no escape. The growls and grunts ahead intensified as the Biters came towards her with increasing speed. She saw several figures moving towards her in the light her mobile threw out and she turned to run. Biters were not exactly known for their speed, but down here, trapped and with her mind numb with fear, the Biters would not need much speed to catch up with her.

She kept running, her heart pounding, trying to ignore the howling coming from the pursuing Biters. She held her mobile up to see what lay ahead and her heart sank. She was approaching a dead end. The Biters were now no more than a dozen feet away. There seemed to be at least three or four of them. For a moment Protima was paralyzed with fear, with the injustice of having her life snuffed out in a sewer. Then a thought came to her. As the Biters shuffled closer, she reached into the package she had been carrying and took out one of the vials Stan had sent. She had no idea if it would work, but if there was even a slim chance she could survive to unmask a conspiracy that had led to the deaths of untold thousands, she would take it.

The nearest Biter was now almost within touching distance and Protima gagged at the stench of decay. She opened the vial and drank its contents in one long swallow. A burning sensation worked its way down her throat, but she did not have much time to contemplate what the liquid was doing to her. A callused and bloody hand grabbed her shoulder and pushed her down. The next thing she felt was the sharp pain of teeth biting down on her arms. The other Biters gathered around her prone body, and as more of them bit into her, Protima screamed again and again. Tears were flowing down her cheeks as she felt her eyes closing. Then she saw no more.

~ * * * ~

Protima opened her eyes and sat up in a panic, expecting the Biters to be still around her. There was no sign of them. Her phone was lying by her side, and when she picked it up, the screen was cracked, but there was still a faint light coming from the display. The battery was likely almost dead and she passed the phone over her body, seeing bloody bite marks all over her upper arms and chest. The blood had largely dried, telling her that she must have been out for several hours at least. The weird thing was that while she was bloody and mangled like a freshly butchered animal, she felt no pain. Had the vaccine worked? She gathered up the courage and spoke out aloud.

'Hello, my name is Protima and I am definitely not a bloody Biter.'

As her own voice echoed back to her in the tunnel, she burst out into uncontrollable laughter. She had not been transformed into a Biter after all! As she began walking down the tunnel, she found her earlier fatigue and hunger had disappeared. She was feeling reinvigorated with a spring in her step. What had the vaccine done to her?

The Biters must have come down into the tunnels somehow, so there must be an exit. She broke into a near-run, eager to escape her underground prison.

After fifteen minutes, she saw light ahead. Part of her was wary that this would turn out to be another hole in the ceiling but she kept going, and soon she saw that it was an opening to the outside world. A small ladder led up to a circular manhole. Protima tucked the package under one arm and climbed up.

After so much time in the darkness, the daylight blinded her. When she forced her eyes open, she saw she was near the Yamuna river, with the Commonwealth Games village to her right and the large Akshardham temple complex a few hundred meters away. She was more than fifteen kilometers away from the India International Center where she had fallen into the underground tunnels. Just how long had she been underground? Her mobile phone was long out of battery and she had lost her watch somewhere down there. Between the extreme fatigue and hunger and the hallucinations brought on by the ganja leaves, she had fuzzy memories of how long she had wandered underground till the Biters found her.

As she looked around, it struck her just how silent it was. Normally, the bridge in front of her would have been full of cars and trucks, honking their horns so much one would be forgiven for believing that was a prerequisite to getting a driver's license. There would have been children flitting around the huts on the side of the road, where their parents would have been hawking whatever they could—motorcycle helmets, coconuts, magazines. The huts were there, but there were no people in sight. Vehicles were strewn all over the bridge as if a child had scattered them around after playing with them and forgotten to put them away. As Protima approached the bridge, she realized that there were people there after all;

it was just that they were not alive any more. The stench of death permeated the whole area and decomposed bodies lay in the cars and on the bridge.

A school bus stood abandoned on the side of the road and Protima wondered if any of the children had made it to safety. She walked closer, and was shocked as she heard a whimper, quickly cut off. Protima called out, 'If you're in there, I mean no harm. Come out and we can help each other.'

Someone moved inside. Her hopes lifted for the first time in days. The prospect of meeting another human being was so exciting that she threw caution to the wind and ran towards the bus. A small girl emerged first, perhaps no more than five years old. Behind her was a young woman. Both were cut and bleeding, but looked to have avoided serious injury. The little girl took a step towards Protima but the woman held her back with a hand on her shoulder, her expression changing to undisguised horror. She screamed and broke out into sobs.

'What's wrong? Are you hurt?'

The little girl was now staring at Protima and she spoke in a hoarse whisper.

'This Biter talks, Mama.'

Protima stopped, stunned at the words. That was when she caught a look at her reflection in one of the bus's windows. A gasp escaped her lips as she realized what had happened to her. She sat down on the ground, stunned. The vaccine. Was this what it had done to her? Death would have been preferable to the monster staring back at her in her reflection. She had not felt any hunger or fatigue after being bitten, and she had thought it had something to do with the vaccine. It perhaps did, because while she could still think and speak like a human, she looked like a Biter. Her eyes were yellowing, and seemed to be devoid of any expression, and when Protima tried to force a smile, she recoiled at the hideous grimace that was reflected back.

It was then that Protima realized another element of her humanity she had lost. Try as she might, she could no longer cry.

Protima jerked her head up as the familiar shuffling of Biters approached. She peered past the side of the bus and saw a crowd of more than a dozen Biters. She flattened herself against the bus, hoping the Biters would pass. The Biters walked on by, emitting growls and screeches, and Protima kept willing them on.

That was when the little girl inside the bus coughed. The Biters stopped in their tracks. Protima was lying flat on the ground, watching from beneath the bus, as one or two took steps towards the bus. One of them, a large man with most of his scalp missing and his face covered in blood, screamed and the others began moving towards the bus. Protima knew what would happen to the girl and her mother if the Biters got to them. If the mother tried fighting back, she would be torn apart, and then the girl would either meet a similar fate or become another monster like the Biters. With all the death and devastation Protima had seen, what was the life of one little girl worth?

With that thought, Protima stopped herself. No, she had to do something, anything. She stepped out from behind the bus and stood between the mob of Biters and the bus.

The large man bared his bloodied teeth and screamed something at her. Protima was shocked as she thought she understood what he was trying to say. He was telling her that the prey inside the bus was his. He towered over Protima as he approached, the others following him. Protima felt around herself for something she could use as a weapon. Her hands felt something hard and she picked it up. She held it above her head and screamed at the Biters.

'Stand back! You will not move forward!'

The Biter was now just feet away from her and her impact on him was immediate. He stepped back as if he had been jolted by electricity. The other Biters had stopped, and one or two of them began to whimper. Perhaps it was seeing someone like them who could talk like a human, or perhaps it was the simple fact that someone had taken charge. Whatever the reason, the Biters began to step back as Protima walked towards them. At any other time, it would have seemed absurd to Protima—a pack of bloodthirsty Biters falling back before a frail old woman—but now she had only one thought in her mind: she had to save the little girl.

The large Biter got up, snarling at Protima, and was about to lunge when Protima swatted him with the object in her hand.

'I said no. No!'

Later, Protima would wonder where she got the courage and strength from, but at that moment she felt as if she could have taken on a dozen Biters in hand-to-hand combat. The Biter shrank before her as she swatted at him again.

Much later, she would come to realize that every pack

needed a leader. She was the first and only Biter who had been able to order them around. The object she was holding would also become a symbol of her authority.

A roaring sound filled the sky as four jets flew towards the city center. They dived in and pulled up in steep dives, and fireballs erupted where their bombs had hit. The government was bombing what had been densely populated civilian areas.

The Biters were still kneeling before her and even the large one was now keeping his head down. She called out to the woman and the girl in the bus, but received no answer. They had slipped out. Protima doubted they could last long, but she had done all she could.

Some figures came into view to her right as a long line of Biters emerged from the nearby fields. They moved as a group now, with some sense of co-ordination. They attacked humans on sight, yet they resembled wild animals more than the monsters people had taken them to be.

Protima began to walk away, not entirely sure where what she would do next. She sensed movement behind her. The Biters were following her.

'Stop following me!'

The Biters stopped, but then they began following her again. Resigned to having the mob of Biters following her around, she kept walking away from the city.

More jets had appeared in the skies and explosions were rocking the city. In the distance, she saw something that froze her heart. A large mushroom cloud was rising into the sky. Protima did not know if this was part of the nuclear madness that had erupted between India and Pakistan or part of the desperate defensive measures adopted by governments to stave off the spread of Biters. Either way, it was clear that it was no longer safe to be above ground. She had already seen that the network of tunnels and sewers under the ground could provide some sort of sanctuary. She laughed bitterly. At least she would not have to worry about finding food or water.

She found an opening and began to pull at the heavy handle. To her surprise, several pairs of hands reached out to help her and in no time, the heavy lid covering the entrance to an underground tunnel was pushed aside. She looked at the Biters following her, now more than two hundred strong, and she saw that they were trying to communicate with her. One of them, a giant who towered over her and wore a hat, growled in a low voice. Protima could not understand the words, but he was telling her that all the Biters would follow her, and that she should lead them to safety. As his eyes scanned the sky, looking at the jets and at the huge fireballs now erupting over the city in the distance, she saw that he and the other Biters were terrified. They might have looked like monsters, but Protima began to understand that there was something more to them. She really did not want to be their leader or to have them follow her around, but there was no way she could turn them back, and besides, with the devastation being rained on the city around them, she did not have much time. So she entered the hole in the ground, and the big Biter with the hat and the others behind him followed her in.

Protima clutched the package she had been carrying close to her and realized she was still carrying the object she had picked up in the stand-off with the Biters. She burst out laughing when she realized what she had been trying to fight off a horde of Biters with.

It was a well-worn and slightly charred copy of a book she had once enjoyed tremendously. Alice in Wonderland.

THE GENERAL'S STRIPES

T HE FIRST SALVO IN THE Chinese Revolution of 2014 was typed into a Google search bar while sipping on a glass of red wine in a five-star hotel in Beijing.

Edward Johnson had come to Beijing on a business trip from his company's China headquarters in Guangzhou two days earlier. Wearing a tan suit and carrying a leather laptop case, he looked like many of the other guests at the East 33 restaurant at the Raffles Beijing Hotel—foreign business travelers staying at the opulent hotel in the heart of the capital. He had been employed with an American electronics firm as a sales director for five years and spoke fluent Mandarin, something that had quickly endeared him to his local Chinese business partners in the year he had been there. He had a doting wife and a five-year-old son, who were now back in the United States taking care of her mother, who had been diagnosed with cancer. Edward's bosses thought him a hard worker, and a stickler for detail, though his evaluations would always call out that he perhaps lacked the leadership to stand out. His Chinese business partners loved his humility and grace, and talked about how despite his senior position, Edward would always be just another member of the team.

Indeed, blending in was critical to Edward's success. For one did not become a professional assassin by attracting attention to oneself.

Edward was indeed on the payroll of the American company, and his immediate bosses had no idea that he was anything but another dedicated middle manager. However, his real employer was Zeus, and he had been placed in China after a four-year mission in the United States where he joined his employers straight out of a commission in the US Army.

Edward, which was not his real name, had been in the US Special Forces, having seen action in Iraq and Afghanistan over multiple tours of duty. He had seen friends torn apart by bombs and rockets and then been ordered not to retaliate because the attackers were 'good' Taliban, on the payroll of supposed US allies in the Kabul regime. He had come to hate how the politicians put young men like him in harm's way and then micro-managed how they could operate. That was till he met Major Appleseed at Kandahar, where Edward had been placed in detention for snapping and shooting dead three civilians. Appleseed had told him he worked for people who wanted to change things, who wanted to take the fight to the real enemies of America. Edward joined in, partly driven by the conviction in Appleseed's words, and partly to avoid the court-martial and disgrace he knew waited for him back in the United States.

Ten minutes ago, he had received a simple text message from his wife. It said, 'The wall near our house is cracked. We should fix it when you're back home.' To anyone intercepting the message, and in China that was always a possibility, it would appear to be innocuous. In reality, it told Edward that the Great Chinese Firewall, which restricted the Internet content available to Chinese citizens, had been taken down. He typed 'Tiananmen Square' into the Google search bar on his smartphone and smiled. A day earlier, the only images he would have been permitted to see would have been those of happy, smiling Chinese citizens strolling in the square. Today, he saw what the rest of the world saw—tanks crushing demonstrators, troops firing into massed youth. Images from the original 1989 massacre and also from the more recent outbreak in late 2012. Edward copied the links and sent out an email from a secure account to a list he already had saved on his phone: a list of the most prominent political dissidents in China. He finished his wine and walked out of the hotel, planning to walk to the nearby Tiananmen Square. He figured he might as well enjoy the square while he could.

~ * * * ~

'Chen, we need you. Please help us out.'

Colonel Chen tried hard to not look into the pleading eyes of his childhood friend, Bo Liang. Liang had been an editor at a local newspaper and a published author and had done very well for himself. The two men, the soldier and the poet, had stayed in touch over the years. That was till Chen had received a notice from the Internal Security Service that he should avoid all contact with his childhood friend since he had been placed under house arrest for 'anti-national activities'. What Liang had done was to post a piece on his blog that had been mildly critical of the force used by the authorities in breaking up the protests in Tiananmen Square in late 2012. Chen had not heard from his friend for some months, and now he had suddenly called him for a meeting at a café. Chen's wife had told him to not go, since he would be watched, but Chen owed his old friend at least that much.

When Chen did not reply, Liang put some printouts on the table.

'Chen, look at these. I had blogged about them killing a few dozen young kids, but it seems they did much more. The Net is open for some reason, and we downloaded these. There was a terrible massacre at Tiananmen, one they hushed up. They took away dozens of people and killed them afterwards. Is this why you joined the army, Chen? To kill your own people?'

At that, Chen's head snapped up. 'Liang, you sit in your cafes and air-conditioned homes and talk of democracy. Look around us and compare to the poverty we ourselves saw as children. See how much our nation has progressed. You talk of democracy—take a look at the United States. Their poor are protesting in the streets and being set upon by hired guns of the elite. With the Occupy protests, many American cities resemble war zones. Europe is in the throes of rioting by unemployed youth and one economy after another is collapsing like a pack of dominos. At least here the Army holds us together against anarchy.'

'Please then, look at this. With the Great Firewall down, we can see what is on the Internet. Please have a look and see the truth for yourself.'

Liang handed a tablet computer to Chen with the browser open to an unfamiliar website. Chen's English was pretty good and he scanned through the page—it was a posting from someone called Dr. Stan on a conspiracy forum. It read, 'The chaos around us is engineered by powerful men. The virus reported in China, the lab fire in Washington everybody is covering up. It will all lead to a catastrophe bigger than anything you can imagine. And don't for a minute think that the wars flaring up around the world are an accident. This is all part of their plan.'

Chen scrolled down and saw that many other posters had responded, most calling the original poster crazy and paranoid. Dr. Stan had never posted again. Chen handed back the tablet, exasperated.

'You expect me to believe this? The ravings of a lunatic on some crazy forum? Seeing stuff like this makes me believe the Great Firewall has its uses after all.'

Chen saw Liang's look of disappointment as he gathered his things and got ready to leave.

'Very well, my old friend. Thank you for coming to meet me. I don't know if we will meet again but good luck.'

With those words, he got up and left. Chen kept looking at the door for some time, wishing he had said something else. But in his heart, he knew he was right. The world was slipping into chaos—the Middle East was on the verge of all-out war between Israel and Iran; the US economy was tottering and social unrest there was boiling over. Closer to home, Islamic insurgents had intensified their campaign in China's Xinxiang province. The war of words with the US over Taiwan had grown sharper, and blood had already been drawn in dogfights over the straits. This was hardly the time when China needed internal strife. Chen knew only too well that the Chinese system was far from perfect, but which system was? At least the nation was prospering, and children in small towns did not have to scrounge for food or an education like his parents had to.

Chen was on leave in Beijing for the next two days, after which he had to report back to his unit near the Indian border. While the two Asian giants enjoyed an uneasy peace, Chen knew just how rapidly that could change. There were dozens of incidents at the border each year, and if it came to a shooting match, Chen and his men would not be facing the ill-equipped infantrymen the Chinese Red Army had smashed through in the 1962 war. The Indian army had grown into a modern army and the fact that both Asian giants now had nuclear weapons made any conflict much more dangerous than it had been in 1962. Chen had found Indian officers to be rational and pragmatic, but what bothered them most was their shared unstable neighbor, Pakistan. If things came to a boil between India and Pakistan, then Chen's leaders would likely ask his troops to take up an offensive posture along the border to tie up India's Mountain Divisions.

With the growing tensions around the world, the last thing Chen wanted was war between India and China. The two Asian neighbors had prospered recently, and a war would set both nations back many years.

Chen was happy to be back home so he could forget about his worries and spend some time with his wife. When he entered his apartment, his wife had already laid out dinner, and he kissed her as he sat down to eat.

After months of eating whatever their cook could rustle up at their post, Chen found the home-cooked food heavenly. He took in the smell of the thick chicken soup and smiled as he tucked into the noodles and steamed dumplings. However, he had barely started his meal when there was a knock on the door. Then another.

Only the Internal Security men would walk up to a senior officer's home and knock like this without being stopped by the security guard in the apartment complex downstairs. He had taken a risk in agreeing to meet Liang, and he hoped he could talk his way out of this.

Chen placed his hand over his wife's before she could rise to answer the door. He spoke in a hoarse whisper.

'Get inside the bedroom and lock the door.'

He kissed her again and ushered her into the bedroom. His pistol was in a drawer, but he knew that if they had indeed come for him, trying to resist would only make things worse. He forced a smile and opened the door to find two men in black suits.

'Comrade Colonel Chen, I'm afraid I have some bad news for you.'

Chen felt his throat tighten but he forced himself to not let his fear show.

'Comrades, come in. What has happened that you needed to come by so late at night?'

One of the men held a black-and-white photograph in front of him. Chen blanched as he saw the two bodies lying in a pool of blood.

'Comrade Colonel, a friend of yours, Bo Liang, met with an unfortunate accident this evening. As far as we can tell, his wife also died with him and we know of no other immediate family. The last dialed numbers on his phone were yours so we thought we would inform you so that you could help make the necessary arrangements.'

~ * * * ~

Edward smiled as he saw his Chinese colleagues talk in hushed whispers in the company cafeteria. There had been only one topic of conversation for the last five days. The Great Firewall was down and the Chinese people were lapping up information from the Internet that had been denied to them for decades. There had been an interruption previously, in early 2012, when the hacker group Anonymous had hacked into a couple of Chinese government websites. But this was on a totally different scale—the entire firewall had been compromised.

The Chinese government had been taken unawares, and at first had tried to avoid any public comment on the situation, but as the days wore on and Facebook and Google+ pages called sprouted calling for political reform and Twitter messages abounded announcingannounced protests against local corruption, the government had been forced to act. The online protests were perhaps something the Chinese regime could have hoped to ignored, but when those led to mass gatherings and protest marches, it had did not have much of a choice but to respond. The response was just as Edward's bosses had hoped. The Chinese regime had dismissed the protests as the work of `misguided terrorists' in the media and had taken in some of the protestors for beatings at police stations. That had further inflamed public opinion.

The TV in the cafeteria had been relaying news of ongoing demonstrations in Guangdong province when a news flash appeared, taking even Edward by surprise. As he listened, he reminded himself that he had no business feeling angry at his masters for not showing him the whole picture. He was a small cog in their plan. As reports emerged of a strange, highly contagious virus in inner Mongolia, with the Chinese government blaming the United States for an act of biological warfare, he realized the plan was far more dangerous than he had ever anticipated.

~ * * * ~

'Comrade Colonel, your men are ready for inspection.'

Chen straightened his back and saluted as his men snapped to attention as one. He felt a strange sense of pride as he saw the assembled men. More than five hundred of his men had been flown into Beijing over the last two days. The rest of his garrison was still at their post, but his superiors had ordered more elite infantry units back to major cities, to deal with 'potential unrest'. Chen hoped he would not have to order his men to march against Chinese civilians, and he wondered if this was a test of his loyalty, given his links to Bo Liang.

The death of his friend still stung. Chen tried to tell himself it had been an accident, but there was a voice in the back of his head telling him things he did not want to hear. For now his men would stay in their barracks near the airport, and Chen had joined them, awaiting the orders that could come at any minute.

The last week had been one of unprecedented chaos.

The Great Firewall had been largely restored, but the damage had been done. Through much of 2011 and 2012, people in smaller towns had been rising up against local corruption and the fact that so many of them had been displaced to make way for the shining symbols of the new China. Many of those had been put down with brutal force. With the Great Firewall down, all those uncomfortable truths came out, and bereaved friends and relatives found a new outlet for their rage and anguish.

The President had made an appearance on live TV, vowing that he would personally crush corruption. He claimed many of the excesses had been committed by local officials without his knowledge. Chen did not doubt that, since he knew how labyrinthine the Chinese bureaucracy could be, but these assurances did not placate ordinary Chinese. Many local government offices had already been sacked and officials beaten up, or worse, and while disturbances were yet to spill over into the larger cities, Chen knew it would take but one spark to set it all alight. A part of Chen's mind also exhorted him to take a stand and to demand justice for the death of his friend, but that voice was quickly hushed by another reminding him that he had his wife and his parents back in the province to think of.

One evening Chen had sat alone and gotten quite drunk. He had told himself that ifIf he had been fifteen years younger, he would have stormed off and demanded justice for what in his heart he knew to be the murder of his friend. But he was almost forty and had a family to think of, so he needed to weigh his actions. What Chen did not realize at the time was that rationalizing one's inaction was the first step in accepting tyranny. You either stood up against tyranny or became a slave to it, there was nothing in between.

That night, he had an unexpected visitor in his room near the barracks. It was General Hong, the man who had trained him at the Academy and who had been his mentor ever since.

'Sir, you could have called me. I would have come.'

The old general waved Chen's objections aside and sat down, producing a bottle of rice wine and a handful of small packets labeled '05 Compressed Food'. Chen smiled as he saw the biscuit packets. These were the battlefield rations of the Chinese infantry—hard, dry biscuits that packed more than a thousand calories with the nourishment making up for the taste.

'Are you going on a march?'

Chen had meant it as a joke, but there was no humor in Hong's eyes as he looked at his protégé. 'We are already at war. We have been sharing these biscuits to remind everyone that we should forget the comforts of the last few years and learn to be soldiers again. Now share a drink with this old man.'

They drank in silence for some minutes, and Chen was increasingly anxious about what his mentor wanted of him. Finally, Hong looked at him.

'In two days' time, officers loyal to me will seize control of key government buildings. We will then announce that the government is working with foreign powers to create the current instability. We will help keep the peace while we can normalize the situation.' The general poured himself another drink, as if he were talking about the weather.

Chen was in turmoil. His long-time mentor was asking him to take part in an armed coup. To disobey all the orders he had followed, to turn against the same leaders he had sworn to defend.

'Sir, you're one of the most decorated officers in the whole People's Liberation Army. How can we turn against the government?'

Hong poured Chen a drink. There was a look of infinite sadness in the old man's eyes.

'Chen, I am fiercely loyal to China and would die for my nation. But I serve the people, not a few rich men and their backers. I believe our President is an honest man and he has been trying to steer our nation towards progress, but there are forces at play who have their own agenda. They are the ones who have been discrediting him and the government. There are those in our own Army and government who have benefitted much by being in power, and there are whispers of outside powers working with them to lead us down a path to war with the Americans.'

'Why would anyone want that? If they drive us to war with the Americans, what does anyone gain?'

Hong looked straight into Chen's eyes, and Chen saw an expression in the general's eyes that he had never seen before—fear.

'I don't know, but that's why we need to help restore some stability and secure the President against the forces plotting against him. Will you join us?'

Chen sat frozen in place. Joining Hong would be a huge leap of faith. His mentor was persuasive as always, and Chen did not quite know how to refuse a man who had been more than a father to him. However, joining

Hong would mean throwing away his career and placing his wife in tremendous danger. He thought back to the photographs of Liang and his wife, and felt his resolve slipping. Having been a combat soldier for much of his adult life, Chen did not fear much for his own personal safety, but the thought of his wife lying on the road after another such `accident' almost paralyzed him with fear. Hong must have sensed what was on his mind.

'Chen, I have other officers to meet, so I will be on my way. I know what I am asking of you, and I would never place you in such a predicament unless our nation was facing extraordinary danger. You will know when the action starts, and your men are one of the most battle-trained units now in the capital. They will ask you to stop us, and I hope we don't have to meet on the battleground.'

With those words, Hong got up and left.

~ * * * ~

Hong's plan never got off the ground. The next morning, a Chinese destroyer attacked a Taiwanese frigate in open seas and sank it with a volley of missiles. A dogfight broke out when Chinese fighter jets attacked two Taiwanese planes that had flown to the scene. The Taiwanese government was pleading for help from the United States, but with tensions escalating between Israel and Iran, US forces were not in a position to intervene.

Chen got a sense of just how confused things were when he realized that the actions of the destroyer and the jets had not been sanctioned by the government. His friends in the government said the President was fuming because the commanders involved had acted without orders to open fire. Perhaps Hong had been right after all about renegade elements driving the nation towards confrontation.

Chen had been ordered with his men to Tiananmen Square where more than five thousand civilians had gathered, protesting human rights violations and asking for criminal action against those who had killed the student protestors at the square in late 2012. Chen had told his men to ensure that the safety switches on their guns were on and to keep a safe distance from the crowd. He did not want a nervous kid to get trigger-happy and start another massacre. He kept hoping that the demonstrators would disperse when the President came to address them, as had been promised.

Chen waited a few more hours as the crowd swelled. He noted with dismay that some were carrying pipes and bottles. The youngsters had started taunting the policemen and troops. Chen intervened quickly, but the situation was volatile and he was afraid that it could explode at any minute.

He had tried calling Hong several times that morning, but had not been able to get through. The local police who were to be the first line of defense seemed terrified and Chen doubted they would hold their lines if there was trouble. If anything, some of the younger policemen showed sympathy towards the protestors.

~ * * * ~

Edward finished his coffee at the café near Tiananmen Square. He looked at the growing crowd and shook his head sadly. He would much rather his mission be achieved with the minimum collateral damage. The Chinese troops were there, just as his bosses had anticipated, and the poorly trained police would bolt at the first sight of trouble. That would leave heavily armed infantry brought in straight from a hostile international border facing agitated civilians. Combat infantry was trained to kill, not detain or disarm civilians. Edward wondered just how well-connected his bosses were; to manipulate things to this extent would require access to the Chinese government. As he climbed up the fire escape behind the café, he knew that he would never know the full story, and he knew better than to ask questions. Curiosity might or might not kill the cat, but it would certainly lead to a short and exciting life.

Once he was on the roof, Edward opened the briefcase he had been carrying. To anyone looking at the contents, his briefcase contained nothing that would have been out of place for an executive on a business trip. Edward moved the files and papers a bit and snapped open a hidden compartment. He took only five minutes to assemble the sniper rifle.

~ * * * ~

Chen's phone rang and he picked it up, relieved to finally hear from Hong.

'Sir, thanks for calling. I've been trying to call you all morning. We are in an impossible situation here and I have no idea why they ordered my men here, but if anything goes wrong, my boys are not trained to handle civil disturbance. I've been thinking of what you said and I wanted to talk to you.'

To Chen's shock, Hong's voice betrayed panic. 'They are on to us. Someone in our group betrayed us, and they are hunting us down. I don't have much time. Take care, my son.'

With those last words, Hong disconnected the line. Chen would have tried calling him back had one of his men not shouted in alarm.

'Sir, someone's shooting the protestors!'

Three protestors lay in expanding pools of blood. Chen looked on in horror as another one fell, a mist of blood spraying from his head. Chen's trained eyes knew immediately that someone from an elevated area to the right was shooting at the protestors, and that they were using a silenced weapon. Chen scanned the buildings with his assault rifle ready in his hands.

There! He saw a glint of light from what could have been a sniper scope. Another protestor fell. Chen turned to his men.

'Make sure none of you fire. If the crowd stirs up, try and hold them back with minimum force. I'm going after that bastard who's shooting.'

Chen began to run towards the building where he had spotted the shooter, but he was too late. Some of the youth in the crowd recovered from their shock and gave vent to their fury.

'Those swine shot us in cold blood. Get them!'

Bricks and bottles began raining down on the police and soon a group of young men charged the policemen. The policemen tried to rally but two of the police fell, victims to the unseen sniper he was racing towards. A policeman thought someone in the crowd had shot his comrade and opened fire with his pistol, shooting two civilians.

After that, nobody could do anything to stop the unfolding bloodbath at Tiananmen Square.

~ * * * ~

Chen was sitting alone, his clothes drenched in sweat and blood and his body bleeding from at least a dozen cuts and scrapes. He had tried to hold his men back, but once the police fired, a few protestors had snatched guns from them and started firing at the troops. The square was littered with bodies. The sniper who had started it all was gone. Chen's wife had been calling him all day to check if he was okay, and he just grunted once in reply and then did not answer any more calls. Hong was nowhere to be found, and many officers loyal to Hong were missing. The massacre at Tiananmen Square had been a smokescreen for a wholesale purge of officers in the Army who were likely to oppose whoever was orchestrating the events overtaking China.

A TV was on in the corner and Chen saw that the entire world was being engulfed by a catastrophe of the likes that had never been seen before. Regional wars were flaring up, and the disease that he had heard of in Mongolia was spreading like wildfire. There were rumors that it transformed people into undead monsters who preyed on human flesh. Chen had dismissed those stories as the product of an overactive imagination, but now he was no longer so sure. The images of mobs of men and women hunting down others and biting them to death would have been horrible enough, but what made it even more terrifying was that the victims came back to life as monsters themselves. Several cities had been overrun by the contagion and Chen wondered if Hong had been right after all, and if there were indeed forces orchestrating such global chaos.

'Comrade, we need to talk.'

Chen looked up to see a young officer, whom he had not met before.

'Comrade Chen, General Hong told me to come to you if his plans were compromised. He is gone, as are most of the officers, but the men are ready, and they just need a leader to follow.'

'Why don't you lead them?'

The man smiled.

'My friend, I am an accountant who has never been in battle, which is why nobody suspects me of being a part of the plan. We need a warrior, not a bean counter, to lead the troops. You surely know now the kind of ruthless men we are up against, and unless we act fast, all will be lost. I don't know what their plan is and what they ultimately want, but they clearly are in the highest reaches of the government and the Army. We must act fast before more innocent lives are lost.'

Chen thought back to the hundreds of lives lost in the square earlier in the day and he looked up at the officer.

'What do I need to do?'.

~ * * * ~

While Chen was sitting in his barracks planning his next move, Edward was at the airport, waiting to catch a flight out to Hong Kong. He had an onward journey booked to New York, where he would dispose of his current identity and take a well-deserved two-month vacation.

He could almost smell the fear in the business-class lounge. Most people were rooted to the TV sets, which were broadcasting details of how the contagion had spread around the world in a matter of days. The monsters now had a name.

Biters.

The major urban centers of China were still free of the scourge, but with air travel carrying tens of millions of people around the world every day, it was but a matter of time before the infection spread. Edward could only guess as to the ultimate aim of the plan but even what little he had seen was beginning to scare him.

There was a commotion outside and one of the airline employees at the reception got up to see what was the matter. When she turned to face the passengers, Edwards saw a look of fear that quickly gave way to a forced smile as she bravely tried to do her job and reassure the passengers.

'Please stay in the lounge, the police will deal with what is happening outside.'

It would never be known how the first Biters entered Beijing. Perhaps a passenger had brought the infection with him; Edward had already read about flights landing full of Biters with the terrified crew having locked themselves in the cockpits. Or perhaps a Biter had come into the city from the countryside. As with all large cities, once the infection took hold, it spread at an astonishing pace.

Edward was at the glass door now. Blood-covered figures in torn clothes rampaged through the terminal. A man behind him screamed at him to lock the door, but when the Biters smashed another lounge's glass doors and walked in, oblivious to the shards, Edward knew that hiding was not an option. He was not going down without a fight.

As the first Biters approached the business-class lounge, he shouted at the waiters to get knives from the kitchen. He armed himself with two carving knives and met the first Biter as he smashed through the glass into the lounge. Edward slashed him across the throat and kicked down the next Biter before stabbing him through the heart. He heard a gurgling noise behind him and turned to see the first Biter get back up, a gaping hole in his neck where blood spurted out. The Biter bared his teeth and advanced on Edward.

Edward dropped the knife, a terror like he had never known before taking hold of him. How did you fight an enemy you could not kill? He closed his eyes and screamed as the Biter grabbed his hand and bit down hard.

~ * * * ~

Chen had fallen asleep within minutes of getting home at three in the morning. However, it was anything but a sound sleep. He kept dreaming of bloodied corpses and of mobs surging towards him. He heard loud booms and for a minute he thought he was dreaming it. Then his wife shook him awake.

'Huahei, look out there!'

Chen looked out the window to see the night sky light up in the distance with bright bursts of flame. As another explosion sent up a crimson plume, he knew what he was looking at—an attack from the air. The explosions seemed to be coming from the direction of the airport. However, there was no return fire. There was no way an enemy could attack the Chinese capital without its formidable anti-aircraft defenses firing back. What was happening? He picked up his phone as it rang. It was an unfamiliar voice, but the words Chen heard electrified him.

'Comrade, the contagion has spread to Beijing. The Biters overran the airport and we had to destroy it from the air. There are more Biters headed to the city. We need you and your unit to deploy now. A truck is on the way to fetch you.'

Chen's wife had turned on the TV and he saw that the contagion had consumed much of the world and now was at the doorsteps of China's major cities. China's lack of freedom worked in its favor now. Unlike major Western cities, the entrances to Chinese cities were closely guarded. With rising tensions, crack Army units had been positioned outside most cities to guard against escalating civil protests, and while nobody had said it out aloud, the real possibility of a military coup. Together with the network of spies in various communities, the Chinese leadership was able to get word of the emerging outbreak before many other nations.

The President was on TV now and Chen felt an emotion he thought he had forgotten—patriotism.

'My fellow people. Today I speak to you as our nation confronts an enemy we have never fought before. Nation after nation has fallen to this scourge, but we will resist till the very end. As I speak, units of the People's Liberation Army are racing to intercept these infected hordes before they breach our major cities. To civilians caught outside major cities, we will be broadcasting safe zones where you can enter the cities and seek sanctuary. Our nation has been divided, but now the time has come for us to unite in facing this threat. If we fight shoulder to shoulder as comrades, we may yet survive. But if we do not, one thing is certain. Our nation will cease to exist.'

Chen passed through a city in panic as he rode to join his unit. People were boarding up their homes and even at five in the morning nervous crowds were gathering outside. One of the young men began to clap as the Army trucks sped past to meet the oncoming hordes of Biters. It was soon taken up by many others, and an old man emerged from a group, wearing a crumpled old uniform with rows of medals on his chest. He caught Chen's eye and shouted out, 'Go get them, boys! All of China depends on you today.'

Chen spent the rest of the ride thinking about everything he had seen and heard. Minutes later, he was in front of his men.

'Sir, I hear we cannot kill these Biters with bullets.'

Chen stormed up to the young infantryman and grabbed his helmet with both hands, pulling him close till his face was inches away.

'If not with bullets, then we will rip their fucking hearts out with our bare hands.'

He loosened his grip on the shaking soldier and addressed all his men now arrayed before him.

'I know many of you have been troubled, and after what happened yesterday, I cannot blame you. There will be a reckoning one day for those innocent lives lost, but now we are all that stands between those monsters and the millions of people in the city. Fight like this is our last day on Earth because it may well be.'

~ * * * ~

The first Biters came within the hour. There were six of them, all dressed in bloody remnants of Army uniforms. Some of his men hesitated to fire at those wearing the uniform so Chen fired on full auto. One of the Biters dropped as several rounds tore into him. Chen lowered his rifle and then recoiled as the fallen Biter got up, blood covering his torso, and joined the others in walking towards the troops. Some men took a step back and Chen knew he had just a few seconds before his men gave into full-scale panic. His men were well trained, but they had never fought an enemy who could not be shot dead.

He had already heard how other units had panicked and tried to run. That never worked. The moment one of them was bitten, the contagion spread, and within minutes, a disciplined platoon of crack troops was turned into bloodthirsty and mindless Biters.

Chen ordered one of his men to fire an RPG and within seconds the rocket snaked out towards the approaching Biters. It exploded in their midst, scattering all but three of them.

'Did we get them?'

Chen did not answer the man who had asked the

question but brought up his rifle scope to his eyes to take a closer look. The Biters who had been torn apart by the rocket were not dead yet. One of them had his leg taken apart by the rocket but his torso was still trying to crawl towards them, his mouth open with blood and drool streaming out of it. Another had lost much of one side of his body, but both halves were flopping around. As horrified as he was, Chen had just learned an important lesson. Even if the Biters could not be killed, they could be stopped.

'Take their legs apart! Aim low and fire on full auto!'

A volley of rifle fire on full automatic targeted the three approaching Biters and all three of them went down, their legs shredded. What remained of them continued to move and wriggle around on the ground, but they were no longer an imminent threat.

'RPG!'

At Chen's command, another rocket streaked out and obliterated what had remained of the Biters. For all Chen knew, their body parts were still moving, but they were not getting any closer and for now, that was victory enough. A cheer went up as his men realized that the enemy they were fighting could be defeated after all. He turned to smile at the men and shouted loudly enough so that they could all hear him.

'Every bastard thinks he's tough till we put a few rounds into him. If they come again, just remember to shoot low and anyone who hits them in the balls gets a drink from me.'

A few chuckled but then his radioman's face turned ashen.

'Sir, scouts are reporting more of them.'

'Deploy into fire teams of six men. One RPG and five riflemen. Shoot only for the legs and then mop them up with rockets.'

As his men began to deploy, he saw the hesitation on his radioman's face.

'What is it?'

'Sir, aerial recon is reporting that there are hundreds of thousands of Biters headed this way. We just got news that Guangzhou has been overrun, and all radio contact has been lost with the city.'

~ * * * ~

'Sir, we are out of bullets for the sniper rifles.'

That was the last thing Chen needed to hear. All day they had picked off Biters at long range with their snipers. He had ten specialized snipers with him, and they had fired and fired again till their fingers bled and their guns overheated to dangerous levels. But Chen had known it would never be enough. The People's Liberation Air Force had been flying all day as well, but China was a vast nation and the PLAAF was already dangerously overextended.

War had broken out in the Middle East, and with all seemingly lost, Iran had launched nuclear missiles at Israel. Chen had heard that the Middle East was now a radioactive wasteland. India and Pakistan were trading blows as well, and then had come the news that some fool in Taiwan had ordered missiles fired at the mainland. The Chinese had retaliated with a fury, unleashing a barrage of missiles and air strikes. What the Biters could not accomplish in terms of wiping out civilization, it seemed humans would finish on their own. But for now, Chen had more immediate concerns. He had heard back from the Air Force that short of using tactical nuclear weapons, there was no way they could hold the Biters back.

The one silver lining was that news had spread along the line on how to stop the Biters. It was simple really.

Aim for the head. Only the head. That was the only thing would bring a Biter down for good.

So Chen's snipers had been busy for over an hour, shooting down hundreds of Biters from more than two kilometers away. The problem was that they were now out of bullets and there were still thousands of Biters shuffling towards Chen's position. Chen ordered his riflemen to take position, but he did not have high hopes. They could not guarantee head shots at long range, and if the Biters could get close enough, he knew they would be overwhelmed by sheer weight of numbers. Chen thought back to his days in the Military Academy and smiled at the irony of it all. The Chinese Red Army had made itself infamous for its near suicidal 'human wave' tactics which had come as such a nasty surprise to the Americans in Korea. Now the same Red Army faced the prospect of being overwhelmed by sheer numbers, but this time the oncoming wave was hardly human.

Some of the men pointed to the sky as two jet fighters swooped in low, releasing bombs over the approaching sea of Biters. As the bombs exploded, a wave of fire expanded from the point of impact. Even from a kilometer away, Chen could feel the extreme heat they unleashed.

'Was it a nuke?' one of the nervous men whispered. No, it was not a nuclear weapon, but a napalm bomb dropped right in the middle of the approaching Biters.

For a few seconds, all that was visible was a wall of fire and Chen heard cheers. Those disappeared when the Biters emerged from behind the flames. Some of the Biters were on fire, yet they shuffled on, stepping over the burnt bodies of their comrades. Any normal army would have collapsed under the firepower unleashed against them and the devastating losses they had suffered, but the Biters were unlike any army Chen had imagined.

Chen sighted his rifle and took aim, sending a bullet through a Biter's head. A couple of men whistled appreciatively at his aim.

Chen tried to put up a brave front and turned to look at his men.

'Just take off their heads. Not much to it.'

A few of his men took aim and fired and a couple of Biters went down from direct hits to the head. It was but a small victory, but Chen knew the war was far from over, and he was no longer sure he would live to see it through to its conclusion.

~ * * * ~

'Blow the bridge.'

Chen watched as the explosive charges were triggered and the bridge went down, taking with it several dozen Biters. It was now almost dark and they had retreated well into the residential areas of Beijing. Any further and the Biters would be among the millions of civilians now cowering inside the city.

There was no counting how many Biters had been destroyed in the fighting that day but they kept coming.

Many Army units had been overrun, further adding to the ranks of the Biters, and finally Chen had received orders to retreat, destroying all bridges and mining all approach roads along the way. A row of tanks in the distance were heading out to meet the Biters, but he doubted they would achieve much. He had already heard tales of tanks that had destroyed hundreds of Biters, then run out of ammunition and gotten bogged down. Heavy armor was of little use against a seemingly never-ending sea of Biters. Once the tanks ran out of ammunition or got bogged down, the Biters would just bypass them and carry on.

The Biters did not seem to feel tiredness, fear or pain. They kept coming, and several more cities had fallen. Beijing, Shanghai and a handful of other cities were still intact, but he had already heard that with Beijing under greater threat, the government had been flown out to Shanghai. His men were dead tired, and terrified. Many of them just wanted to get home to their families, and Chen thought of his own wife. Yet he knew that he could not allow them to leave their posts. One or two units further to the East had scattered and Chen had heard about several desperate last stands by small units. A dozen men could not hope to last long against the Biters.

Chen had managed to keep his men operating as a cohesive unit, and other than four men who had died when one of their RPGs misfired, he had suffered no other deaths. Most of his men were however dehydrated, and many of them had swollen and bloodied fingers from the constant firing. More than a dozen were wounded due to misfirings and weapons that had overheated, and in more than one case, exploded. Chen had tended to some of the wounded himself, and his uniform was soaked in blood.

For all that, Chen looked at his boys with pride. They had not broken and run as had so many units. For all their misgivings about the regime and their role in Tiananmen Square, they had done their duty to the people of China. They had fought the battle of their lives, not for a flag, not for politicians, but for the millions of ordinary people who counted on them. So, despite every muscle in his body screaming in protest, Chen walked among his men, whispering words of encouragement to each one.

When he was done, he sat down heavily and looked across the river. The horizon was dark with Biters. It was a matter of hours before they reached Beijing and he was not sure they would be able to hold them.

Chen drank some water and thought of how much the world had changed in just one day. Much of the world was lying devastated. The Middle East was largely gone, wiped out in a day of tit-for-tat nuclear exchanges. India and Pakistan had traded their own nuclear blows and their major cities had been hit. Biters had swept through much of the world, and it was unclear if there was any organized government left. In all the chaos, the Great Firewall was down, but as Chen looked at the laptop screen in front of him, he realized news from around the world had not been updated for over six hours.

The latest updates chilled him. The US Government had decided to use tactical nuclear weapons, air burst weapons, on cities that had been totally overrun by Biters. Other nuclear powers—Britain, France, Russia and India—had followed suit. It was a desperate last measure to deny the Biters control over human cities. Chen wondered how many hundreds of millions had died in one day around the world.

One of his men started sobbing and Chen looked up sharply, planning to give the man a lecture. Instead, Chen just stared at the sight he saw, and tears began to stream down his cheeks. Just over the horizon, four giant mushroom clouds billowed over the earth.

~ * * * ~

'There is someone here to see you.'

Chen sat upright, sweat pouring off his face, and his wife placed a gentle hand on his chest, trying to calm him. There were a dozen people sharing their apartment, and many of them looked on as Chen got up to see who was at the door.

With the people that had streamed into the city, Beijing was now home to more than thirty million people, and residents had opened their homes to the newcomers. Three days had passed since Chen and his men had held the line long enough for tactical nuclear weapons to be used to finally secure Beijing. There was no telling whether more Biters would come. China had been home to well over a billion people and only a hundred million were reckoned to be safe. But for now, they had bought themselves some time. Enough time to airdrop thousands of mines around the cities and to ring Beijing and Shanghai with armored forces to hold any further attacks.

It was now a foregone conclusion that any further massed attack by Biters would be met with nuclear strikes. There was no news from the outside world. The Internet was now down, as were phone lines.

A man in a black uniform was waiting for him.

'Sir, I am to get you to Shanghai immediately.'

A few hours later, Chen was waiting in front of a nondescript office in Shanghai. He had put on his uniform, since he was meeting someone at the very top of the government, but he was beyond caring about the reek of sweat and dirt, the tears in a couple of places, or the dried blood all over the front.

The door opened, and he was ushered in. Two old Chinese men were seated at a table, and next to them, surprisingly enough, was a Caucasian man. One of the Chinese men, an old man with ribbons across his chest, nodded at Chen and asked him to sit down.

'Comrade Chen, we thank you for your heroic actions in helping to secure Beijing. Now only Beijing and Shanghai remain, but we will make a new beginning, thanks to the bravery and sacrifice of men like you.'

Chen swallowed hard as the rumors he had heard were confirmed. Only two cities remained intact in all of China. True, that meant that perhaps a hundred million or more had survived, but what about the billion more who were not inside the secure cities? How many billions had perished or become Biters around the world?

The old man continued. 'In the chaos, we suffered terribly. The President and his cabinet perished in an air crash as they were being flown to Shanghai, and so now we are trying to re-establish order. As you can see, we are putting past differences aside and are joining hands with like-minded American friends. Together we will usher in a New World and begin afresh. Our nation, our civilization, is the only one left intact from all the nations of old, and we will begin to spread civilization again through the world. Unfortunate as the circumstances are, perhaps it is our destiny to be the ones who reclaim our planet in the name of human civilization. But first, we must secure our cities and feed the millions of civilians that depend on us. For that we need men like you.'

'Comrade, what could I do to help?'

The second Chinese man spoke.

'We are bringing the old government and armed forces into one single command structure, called the Central Committee. We need our Chinese soldiers to keep order in our cities, but we will need other forces to seek out survivors in other parts of the world and to secure resources and food for our people. In that, we will be helped by the forces that our American friends have at their disposal. A highly trained force called Zeus. We will bring their forces and ours into one command, and we need capable men to lead them. Our aerial reconnaissance indicates that there are two major areas where there may still be land to grow food and where there may still be human survivors who need our help— the Midwest of North America and the Northern plains of India.'

After all that he had seen over the last few days, Chen replied without a second thought, 'Comrade, where can I serve and who do I report to?'

The old man chuckled.

'You are everything I had read about you—a committed soldier to the core. No, Comrade, your days of reporting to others are over. As of today, you are a General.'

The man stepped forward and pinned a medal on

Chen's chest, and a set of stripes on his shoulders. Chen was too stunned to say anything.

'Comrade General Chen, welcome to the Red Guards.'

A BUNNY'S LAST WISH

'**O**F ALL THE THINGS ANYBODY has ever done to impress a girl, dressing up as a bunny must be the weirdest and stupidest plan. I do hope she's worth it.'

Neil smiled and playfully threw some water from the sink at Jiten. 'She is not just any girl. She is the one.'

Jiten shook his head. 'Dude, I hear you and I'm sure she's special but please take a look at us. She's rich, she's good-looking and we spend our spare time serving pizzas and washing dishes.'

Neil was not dissuaded. He had heard it all before, and it did not bother him. He might not have had much, but one thing he did have was boatloads of determination. He was only eighteen, but having grown up in an orphanage had matured him much faster than others his age. He had quickly learned that if he wanted to do something with his life, he would need two things—education and money. So he had studied his butt off and got admission into one of the best colleges in New Delhi, and he worked two part-time jobs to pay the fees and save up for a professional degree. He did not know much about what was expected or even whether he would be good at it, but his dream was to get an MBA. For Neil, it was simple—he wanted a job. A job that made sure he no longer had to worry about money; a job that helped him get rid of the label of being a nobody that he had carried ever since he had been born; a job that paid him enough and gave him enough respectability for someone like Neha.

But for now, he still had to get her to date him. The very first time he had seen her, up on stage during a college function, he could have sworn a voice whispered into his ears that she was the one. He had had his share of crushes, but with Neha, it was different. He would hang around after class, whiling away time over cups of tea so that he could see her finish her class and get into her chauffeur-driven car. He signed up for an extra credit in Philosophy and suffered through incomprehensible lectures on Kant and Plato just so he could sit behind her. Of course, she had never noticed him. Neha was one of the most popular people on campus, and he was an outsider. Most of the kids came from privileged families, with cars, flashy phones and late-night parties they attended together. He was the poor orphan from a different world.

With half the college queuing up to be Neha's boyfriend, on the face of it, Neil's chances were slim. But he was not one to give up so easily. So a few Google searches later, he had found out something that nobody else knew. Neha was a volunteer for the Make-A-Wish foundation, and so Neil had offered to volunteer there as well. Six months had passed, and then he had been called up for his first wish—to accompany a five-year-old with leukemia to meet her favorite movie star. The movie star had agreed and Neil and another Wish Granter were to accompany the child and her family from their humble home on the outskirts of Delhi to meet the star in a hotel.

When Neil had first seen the little girl with her hair all gone to multiple sessions of chemotherapy, something in him changed. He realized that while he had started this all as a ruse to get closer to Neha, he wanted passionately to help these kids—to give them the joy that came with fulfilling their wishes, to bring some hope into their lives, if even for a day. Joy and hope that nobody had brought into his when he was growing up in the orphanage. Every time one of the kids smiled, it felt like in some way he was making up for all the nights he had cried himself to sleep at the orphanage. So he had dived into his volunteer work with a vengeance and in the New Year's party, he was given an award for being the most active and enthusiastic Wish Granter in all of Delhi.

That day, Neil learned another lesson—that sometimes just doing what was right eventually got you more reward than any amount of scheming and planning. He sat at the same table as Neha that night, and they immediately hit it off. She saw not another boy from college wanting to get into her pants, but a gentle, sincere boy who gave so much of his time for a cause she so dearly loved. Neil learned that Neha had lost her mother to cancer, which had made her embrace the work of the Make-A-Wish foundation with such fervor. They stayed in touch, and within days, Neil got the news that for the next wish, he was to partner with Neha. In some secret corner of his mind, he wished that Neha had requested specifically for him to be her partner. The more prosaic truth was the

Wish Granter paired with her had fallen sick and they had picked Neil at random, but that did not bother Neil; he saw this as a sign from God that the wheels were finally turning in his favor.

Of course, that also meant that he had to go dressed as a giant bunny. It seemed that the little girl they were to help that day was a huge fan of the book Alice in Wonderland, and wanted Wonderland to be enacted for her. She was to be dressed as Alice, Neha was to be the Queen, and of course, Neil was to play the part of the role of the rabbit who led Alice down the hole. Neil knew he looked silly in the oversized bunny ears. He was tall and lanky to the point of looking gaunt, and the large, floppy ears only made him look even taller and thinner. But it would make a sick little girl smile, and yes, it would allow him to spend time with Neha. After the wish, he had planned on asking her out for a coffee, and pleasant thoughts of their first date occupied him as he rode his bike to the girl's home, where he and Neha were to prepare a Wonderland-themed birthday party for the girl and her friends.

~ * * * ~

Neil had been riding his bike for almost thirty minutes when he first got a sense that something was wrong. Normally, in the middle of a Saturday afternoon, traffic should not have been so bad, but now cars were backed up as far as he could see. The girl's home was in a compound of low-rise apartments just a few kilometers away from where he was now, near the Delhi zoo, but with the state of traffic that he saw around him, there was no way he was going to make it in time.

Loud music sounded to his right and an auto-rickshaw pulled up. The driver was smiling and singing along, and when he saw Neil stare at him, he turned the music down. 'Don't look so serious, young man. We'll be stuck here for quite some time.'

'Why, is there an accident or something up ahead?'

The auto-rickshaw driver looked at Neil as if he were an idiot. 'Don't you watch the news? The demons are loose now. I hear they think the bloody Delhi Police will stop them. All they know is how to take bribes.'

Neil leaned closer to see what the man was talking about, and caught a whiff of country liquor. There was a half-empty bottle nestled against the man's legs. No wonder he was babbling about demons. The man saw Neil's expression and pointed to the bottle. 'My friend, you also go and get a good drink before the demons come.'

One of the cars inched forward, and Neil maneuvered his bike through the gap. He managed in this fashion for a few minutes, moving perhaps a few hundred meters, when he saw that the road ahead was blocked by a police jeep. Three nervous-looking constables were standing in the middle of the road, diverting traffic. Not able to move further on his bike, Neil got off his bike and walked towards them.

'What's happening? Why are you blocking the traffic?'

One of the policemen, a kind-looking old man who looked like he had been pulled out of retirement, stepped forward.

'Son, we're just following orders. It seems there's trouble up ahead near the Taj hotel. Officially they haven't told us what's going on yet, but if I were you I would go and spend this time with your family.'

Neil thought back to what had happened in Mumbai a few years earlier when terrorists had attacked a number of hotels and other targets. His heart sank since he knew that Neha's home was close to the Taj.

81

'Is there a terror attack going on?'

The policeman shook his head.

'No, son, it's worse. Have you been following the news about the strange disease that showed up in China?'

Neil got most of his information from the Internet, and sure, he had heard about how a new virus was supposedly taking hold, and how some people were spooked about it. But then, that was the media's job, right? To make everything seem like the end of the bloody world was in sight. He still remembered how they had drummed up SARS, mad cow, bird flu and God knew how many other epidemics that were supposedly going to kill millions, and of course, nothing happened. Plus, the news from the US was just a day or two old—surely no virus could spread so fast? And even if it did, why would the cops be so paranoid?

He took out his phone to call Neha to check what was going on. There were several unread notifications on his Facebook and Twitter icons. As he watched, the count seemed to increase steadily. With slightly shaking hands, he opened up Facebook and scrolled through the status updates of his friends.

'What the hell is going on in Delhi? Isn't traffic bad enough on normal days?'

'They say it's a virus? I think the only virus has affected the traffic lights.'

'Maybe the cops just want some bribes to let us through. Recession must be hard on them as well. ☺'

But then the messages started getting more somber.

'My bro came home and says he saw something on the road near his school. He won't stop crying and he's scared stiff. WTF is going on, please?'

'I stepped out to buy some Coke and the cops are now telling everyone to stay in their houses and lock their doors. Are there terrorists around?'

'Stay safe, guys. The government has declared a state of emergency. How can they do that without even telling us what's going on?'

'One of the news channels got an interview with a guest at the Taj. He was babbling about monsters.'

At that point, Neil stopped, a knot forming in his stomach. He had dismissed the auto-rickshaw driver's comments as the rants of a drunk, but what was really going on? What was this talk of monsters?

Then he saw the status update that galvanized him into action. It was from Neha.

'I'm scared. I can see these... things... walking outside. There are some cops firing at them. I'm alone and my dad's at work. Don't know what to do.'

Neha was alone, and in danger. Monsters or no monsters, Neil was not going to leave her alone at a time like this. He responded to her update with a simple comment.

'I'm coming for you.'

He revved his bike and tore through the police barrier. One of the cops grabbed at the bag that contained his props and in the struggle, managed to snatch the bag away, leaving just the large bunny ears in Neil's hands. Needing both hands free to control his bike, Neil put the ears on top of his head and rode off towards Neha's home as fast as he could.

A thin boy wearing pink bunny ears was hardly the sort of one-man army movies or novels would portray, but today Neil George was angry enough to go to war with anyone who was threatening Neha.

~ * * * ~

Neil didn't have to go far before he saw the first signs of trouble. He needed to take a right turn near the Old Fort to get to Neha's home, but the road was blocked by people running across the road from the government colonies to the left. Many of them were well-dressed and perhaps the families of the officials who stayed in the apartments, but there were also some pavement dwellers and even some policemen. One of the policemen took one look at Neil and shouted, 'Have you lost your mind? Don't go any further.'

Neil didn't have time to ask anyone what was happening, since the crowd seemed to be seized with a wild panic. While he waited for them to pass, he took a quick look at his phone. There was a new update on Neha's Facebook page: 'Neil, don't come here. They are all around.'

Neil started his bike and rode straight past the fleeing crowd. Neha was clearly in great danger and he was not going to leave her.

Neil had progressed only a half-kilometer further when he first saw them.

An elderly man staggered to the side of the road, blood all over his clothes. His white hair was covered in red and his face was barely visible behind a mask of blood. The man was moving slowly, as if in immense pain, and before he could consciously think about it, Neil had stopped the bike near the old man.

'Do you need help?'

The man's head snapped up and Neil realized that something was terribly wrong. The man's eyes were yellow and vacant and his lips were drawn back, making him look more like a snarling dog than a human being.

Neil noticed the foul smell, like that of dead rats, and he wondered what was wrong with the old man. That was when the man growled and lunged at Neil, trying to bite him.

'Holy shit!' Neil almost fell off his bike in terror but recovered his wits in time to start his bike and speed away. Now other bloodied figures emerged from the colony. They were all shuffling along in a slow gait and as Neil caught a glimpse at one or two of their faces, he saw the same lack of expression. They snapped and clawed at him with their teeth or clawing in the air as he passed.

Neil was more scared than he had ever been in his life. What the auto-rickshaw driver had said came back to him and he wondered if these were actually demons. A couple of the Facebook posts had said that someone in the government had announced that this was the result of the virus that everyone had heard about sweeping through the US, but Neil wondered how a virus could possibly turn people into the inhuman wraiths he saw all around him.

He swerved his bike to the right just in time to avoid three of them coming at him and rode down a side street. An overweight man ran onto the streets and right into the path of the three Neil had dodged. One of them clawed at the fat man's face, drawing blood. As the man clutched his bloodied face, another one bit into his shoulder. Blood spurted out in a fountain and the man went to his knees, as another one of his attackers bit him.

When Neil found an isolated patch hidden by a clump of trees, he stopped his bike. He retched and retched again as he remembered the blood, the fat man screaming as he was bitten and the sickening fetid odor.

Neil sat there for some time, wondering what was going on. Just then, his phone rang. It was Neha.

'Neil, please don't come here. They're calling them Biters. They attack any person they see, and once they bite you, you become like them in a few hours. They're saying on TV that the government is trying to quarantine parts of the city to contain the spread of the virus.'

'Where are you, Neha? Are you okay?'

'I'm hiding in our apartment. The Biters are all around the colony and I don't think they've seen me yet.'

Hearing Neha's terrified voice was like a splash of cold water. Neil was still scared, he still did not understand how a virus could have caused so much carnage, and he didn't know how he was going to get through the rampaging Biters to get to Neha's home. But hearing her gave him something to focus on, something that took his mind away from just how terrified he felt.

'Neha, stay there. I'm less than a kilometer away, and I'm coming to get you.'

~ * * * ~

Around the next corner, Neil saw a scene straight out of a movie. An aging policeman was standing with a rifle in his hand, shepherding dozens of terrified people into a high-rise apartment building. Neil had no idea if that guaranteed them any safety against the Biters, but in a city where everyone seemed to have lost their mind, this one policeman's selfless act of bravery stuck a chord.

A crowd of Biters, at least twenty strong, advanced towards the policeman, who had by now sent the last of the civilians into the building and turned to face the Biters. Neil had slowed his bike down, waiting to see what happened, praying that perhaps the policeman would stand a chance. The Biters were advancing, fanning out like a pack of animals to encircle their prey. The policeman showed no sign of panic, indeed he moved deliberately, and with, for lack of a better word, dignity. He knelt and brought his rifle up to his shoulder. As the Biters came in even closer, Neil sent up a silent prayer for the old man.

The policeman fired and Neil smiled as one Biter went down, spurting blood from a direct hit to the chest. The policeman fired again, and another Biter went down, this time with a gaping neck wound. The policeman might have been incredibly brave, but he was certainly not suicidal. Neil saw that he was buying time, and with every shot was moving closer to the building where the door was still ajar, and those he had saved were cheering him on. The old man fired twice more and two more Biters went down.

Then Neil saw something that in one fell swoop took away all the hope he had harbored. The first Biter who had been shot was now sitting up, and despite the bloody mess on his chest, got up and began walking towards the policeman. The second Biter, with a grotesque hole where his neck should have been and his head hanging slightly to one side, was also sitting up. The policeman dropped his rifle and Neil could see that the old man's lips were moving rapidly in prayer, but there would be no saving him today. The Biters ripped into him in a frenzy, and they tore the policeman apart till there was nothing but a mess on the road.

The people shut the door but the Biters were banging on it, and Neil knew it would be a matter of time before the door gave way. Something snapped inside Neil, and he felt a surge of anger. He picked up a metal rod lying on the side of the road and drove his bike as fast as he could towards the Biters. He swung the rod with all his strength. It connected with a satisfying thud and a Biter fell, his head smashed in. He did not get back up. Neil knew he did not stand a chance against all the Biters, but, having extracted revenge for the policeman's sacrifice, he swerved away towards Neha's home, the rod now tucked under his arm.

Most roads were blocked by bands of Biters and he took another detour through the normally busy Khan Market toward Neha's place. The market was deserted, other than Biters roaming around and bodies lying in the street. That was when he saw a group of Biters crouching over a prone figure. It was a thin, elderly woman, and she seemed paralyzed with fear, clutching a large package to her chest. Neil swooped in, and once again, his rod did its work, splattering the brains of a Biter on the pavement.

'Come on!' Neil grabbed the old woman with one hand and pulled her towards him. She seemed to have recovered her wits a bit and sat behind him as he sped away. She was mumbling something, clearly in shock.

'Look, I need to get to my girlfriend's place. Where can I drop you?'

There was no reply, and Neil was beginning to get irritated, knowing that every second with her was a second wasted.

'You must have a home or a family somewhere?'

The woman just sobbed, and Neil realized that he was perhaps being too tough on her.

'I'm sorry. Things are crazy and I just want to make sure she's okay. I'll drop you wherever you want, just tell me where.'

She looked at Neil, and he saw not just fear, but sadness in her eyes, as if she had lost something or someone of immense value. 'Young man, you have done quite enough for me. Just drop me ahead near the India International Center. It doesn't yet look overrun and I can see a lot of policemen in front of it.'

He took her near the gate and as she dismounted, he smiled.

'There must be something really important in that packet you're carrying. You didn't let go.'

As she walked into the Center, Neil turned his bike and drove towards Neha's home, hoping she was still okay and wondering if he would be able to protect her.

~ * * * ~

The last few hours had been so chaotic that Neil had almost run straight into the dozen or so Biters now crossing the road. Neil ditched his bike just in time and lay flat on the grass near the sidewalk. If he had not been so terrified, he might have found it amusing. The Biters were crossing the road single file, slowly, deliberately, displaying better traffic-safety consciousness than the good citizens of Delhi.

For the first time, Neil got a longer look at the Biters, and he was surprised at what he saw. In the initial chaos, the Biters had seemed rabid, attacking people at random. He now saw that they were moving with some sort of co-ordination. The group that had just passed had perhaps been members of one family or one neighborhood, and seemed to be moving together, with the adults in front and back and children in the middle.

Before proceeding to Neha's home, Neil fished out his phone and checked the news. What he saw froze his heart.

There were unconfirmed reports of nuclear war in the Middle East and tactical nuclear exchanges between India and Pakistan had already taken place. North Korea had lobbed missiles armed with chemical weapons at Seoul and Taiwan and the Chinese mainland were trading missile strikes. Biters were roaming freely in all major cities in the world and most governments seemed paralyzed by the sudden chaos. What had begun as an outbreak of some sort of deadly virus was heading towards a climax where the world melted in a nuclear holocaust.

Neil clicked on the Facebook icon and saw that updates were now scarce. People were perhaps just too busy trying to stay alive... or... Neil didn't want to contemplate what might have happened. A day earlier, they had been sharing an update on their new dress, or a bad grade in a test, or their mood. There were a couple of updates on the page of Make-A-Wish India, one posted by Dr. Joanne Gladwell, who was one of the senior volunteers at the foundation and took care of a lot of their fundraising activities.

'Calling all friends. The US Embassy staff and families are all headed to a safe zone near the Domestic Airport. The Indian Army has secured the area and is calling on all civilians to head there.'

The airport was at least an hour's ride away, and Neil considered the corpse-littered street ahead of him. He could just get on his bike and make straight for the airport. The Biters, as horrifying as they were, did not move too fast, so there was a good chance that he could get there in safety. Or he could still try and get to Neha. He weighed it for a few seconds. Sure, he had called Neha his girlfriend to the old woman, but that was wishful thinking. Neha was someone he had a bad crush on, but to be perfectly honest, she was not even a close friend. He looked at the last update from Neha on Facebook.

'Neil, they are in the apartment downstairs! Don't come, please. I want you to be safe.'

That made up Neil's mind for him. Here he was, worrying about his pathetic little life, and there was Neha, in imminent danger, trying to keep him safe. It did not matter whether she was his girlfriend or indeed, whether they would ever get a chance to form any sort of relationship. There was a relationship bigger than one formed by love, lust or relation. That was the fact that they were all human, and if people were to have any chance of surviving, they would have to stick their necks out for each other.

Neil hefted the metal rod in his hands. Till that morning, he had never struck another person, even in a schoolyard scrap. Neil had always been the one to walk away. Other boys in the orphanage had only paid lip service to the sermons doled out by the Catholic nuns who ran it, but without a family or much to call his own, Neil had embraced their teachings. He wondered how what he was seeing around him squared with all that he had been taught about good and evil. In his young mind he reconciled himself to the fact that the devastation unfolding around the world was a sign of the End Times, and that now was the time when good and pious people would have to step up and help others.

He waited till the last of the Biters was out sight and then mounted his bike for the last stretch of his ride to Neha's home.

~ * * * ~

Neil had been a pretty keen cricket player as a child, and he tried to block out the blood and splattered brains, instead pretending that he was playing a game of cricket and dispatching each delivery out of sight. He held the thick metal rod in a two-handed grip, almost perpendicular to his body, in a stance that would have been more at home on a baseball diamond than a cricket pitch, and waded into the Biters outside Neha's home.

He had arrived to find a good half-dozen Biters clawing at the door to the stairwell that led up to her apartment. The apartment downstairs had been torn apart, and other than huge bloodstains around the floor there was no sign of the inhabitants. The rod made solid contact with another Biter's head, this one a middle-aged woman who had an iPod dangling around her chest, the earbuds still in her ears. As the Biter fell, her head cracked open and Neil took a breather. Fueled by rage and adrenaline, he had waded into the Biters, and now three of them lay at his feet. But that still left three more closing in on him, drooling and growling, and his shoulder felt like it was on fire. He resolved that if he got out alive, and if anyone made movies ever again, he'd write to them telling them just how unrealistic their fight sequences were. He could barely breathe, and had to muster every single ounce of strength left in him to lift up the rod again and smash it against a Biter's head. He missed but made solid contact with his shoulder. The Biter, a big man in a bloody, torn vest, roared and clawed at Neil's hand, drawing blood.

'Shit!'

Neil looked at the growing trickle of blood on his forearm and backed away. He had no idea if the virus or whatever made people into ghouls could be transmitted by a scratch, but he figured he would find out soon enough.

'Sissies scratch. Men do this!' The normally mild-mannered Neil's face was a mask of rage as he swung his rod again and smashed open the Biter's head. The two remaining Biters looked down at the carnage around them, and for a second, Neil hoped that they would decide to cut their losses and find easier prey. Instead, they roared in fury and advanced on him again.

In his duels so far, Neil had learnt an important lesson. He could break their hands, smash their knees, crack open their ribs, but they would keep coming. The only thing that stopped them was smashing open their heads. So he had quickly overcome his squeamishness and started aiming only for the head. The first time he had made solid contact and taken off a Biter's head, he had screamed aloud.

'Off with their heads!'

Wearing his bunny ears and having set out to enact Alice in Wonderland, he though it only appropriate and he was repeating that battle cry as he took on the remaining Biters.

The rod he was carrying was covered with blood and other gore that Neil did not want to think about. Neil swung his rod at one of the remaining two Biters and missed, slipping on the blood on the floor. He tried to recover his footing but fell hard on his back, the rod rolling a few feet away. Neil backed away as the two Biters steadily advanced on him. Both had their blood-stained teeth bared and were a mere couple of feet away when they staggered back as a thick foam enveloped them. Neha stood in the doorway, a portable fire extinguisher in her hands. She sprayed the Biters again and then screamed at Neil.

'Come on!'

He grabbed the rod and the two of them ran out of the apartment building, leaving the two Biters behind. Neha got on the bike behind Neil and they sped away.

'Where do we go now?'

Neil knew the answer to that. The problem was getting there in the fading light with millions of Biters rampaging through the streets of Delhi.

~ * * * ~

They had stopped at an abandoned gas station to top up Neil's bike for the remainder of the ride to the airport. In the twenty minutes since they had left Neha's home, they had seen plenty of Biters roaming in the streets, but moving at speed, they had managed to get this far without incident. The remainder of the trip to the airport would require them to get on the highway, where Neil hoped they could pass unmolested, but they would not have many opportunities to top up his fuel tank, which was nearing empty. So he had taken the risk of stopping to pump gas into the bike, the rod that had served him so well in his other hand. Neil caught a glimpse in the mirror ahead of him, and he scowled.

'I forgot I'm still wearing these silly bunny ears.'

He was about to take them off when Neha's hand gently tousled his hair. Her touch sent a jolt through him.

'I think you look cute in these.'

Neha laughed but then Neil noticed a change in her tone as she touched his shoulder.

'Neil, you're bleeding!'

Neil looked at his hand, still bloody from the scratch he had suffered at Neha's apartment. 'Relax, it's just a scratch.'

'No, I mean up here.'

Neil caught the tension in her voice and took a look in the mirror near him. There was a red patch on his left shoulder. He dropped the rod and peeled back his shirt. His shoulder was covered in a thin film of blood. He wiped some of it away to reveal puncture wounds.

'Neil, did they get close enough to...'

Neha did not dare complete the sentence, but the moment Neil saw the wound, the same thought had burned itself into his mind. Had he been bitten? He could not remember it, but then the struggle below Neha's apartment had been so savage that he had not really been conscious of much other than swinging his rod at the nearest Biter he could see. He had assumed the pain in his shoulder was from the exertion of the fight. But now, looking at the wound, he was beginning to have doubts. He looked at Neha, his eyes filling with tears.

'How long do I have? Have you read anything on the Internet?'

He could see that Neha was starting to cry as well and sobs racked her body as she tried to turn away. 'Maybe it's just a cut.'

Neil got up, holding her shoulders so that she was forced to look straight into his eyes. 'How long do I have?'

Neha spoke in little more than a whisper, seemingly forcing each word out. 'They say that the speed at which the infection takes hold depends on how deep the bite is and the number of bites. Some people with minor bites thought they had got away but became Biters after three or four hours. People who are bitten repeatedly turn pretty much immediately.'

Neil looked at his watch. He had been bitten perhaps thirty minutes ago. Even assuming he had a couple of hours, the best he could hope was to get Neha to the safety of the airport, and then what? He had met many brave boys and girls during his work with Make-A-Wish, and he had marveled at their strength in the face of terminal illnesses. He found his knees buckling and realized that he did not have that same strength. Of course, they had months or perhaps years to go—he did not even have one day.

He just sat there for a few seconds, Neha squatting in front of him, her hands on his shoulders. His mind was numb, with fear, with self-pity, with regret for all the things he would never be able to do. He looked up into Neha's tear-filled eyes, and felt a renewed resolve. Neha must have seen the change in his expression.

'What's wrong?'

He stood up, and finished filling his bike's tank, and then looked at Neha.

'If I drive really fast, I can probably get you to the airport in thirty minutes. So we should still have time before anything happens to me. But before that, will you grant me one last wish?'

Neha burst into tears. 'Neil, maybe it's just a cut...'

Neil held her shoulders and she hugged him.

'You know better than that. Now, we don't have a lot of time. Will you fulfill my wish?'

Neha fought back her tears and nodded.

'I was thinking of asking you out for a coffee after the party today. Will you go out with me on a date? I don't have much money, I don't look like much, but I do have these funky bunny ears and I am currently the world champion in the game of Biter Swatting with my rod here.'

Neha laughed and hugged him tight.

'Lead the way, my bunny-eared hero. Where shall we have our date?'

And so they sat in an abandoned Pizza Hut. They didn't eat or drink anything, but just sitting there, holding hands, made Neil forget, if only for a moment, what he was faced with. For that fleeting moment, he was living his dream.

They talked about their families, their dreams. Neil told her about how he was saving up to go to a good college, maybe get an MBA. Neha told him about how she hated being always told what to do, and being expected to join the family business after an MBA, and how she would much rather become a journalist. They talked about their likes and dislikes, about movies, and music, and friends at college, and then Neil took a look at his watch. It had been just fifteen minutes. The most magical fifteen minutes of his life. But now he had to get Neha to safety. He got up, but she stopped him.

'Your wish isn't yet over. There's something left.'

Then she leaned close and kissed Neil.

~ * * * ~

The highway looked like a giant junkyard, with abandoned vehicles littering it. There were bodies strewn among them, but Neil tried to focus on the path ahead as he maneuvered his bike between the vehicles. They had seen groups of Biters when they had left the city center and taken the road to the highway, but they have been traveling too fast for the Biters to catch them. Now, hemmed in by abandoned cars on all sides, and in the fading light, he was forced to trade speed for safety, and there was no telling what lurked behind the next car. Neha was acting as the lookout, and once or twice she yelled out warnings of approaching Biters, but in both cases, it turned out to be a case of nerves, made worse by shadows being thrown around them.

Then she screamed, but even before the words left her mouth, Neil saw the danger. Two Biters had come out from behind a car to their right. With three abandoned cars blocking the way to their left, they did not have enough room to avoid them. One of the Biters was a frail old man with his face largely ripped off below the nose. The other was a younger man, wearing a bloodied

Mickey Mouse t-shirt. Neil told Neha to be ready to grab the handlebars when he told her to, and then accelerated his bike, speeding towards the Biters. He turned the bike sideways at the last moment and kicked out at the older Biter. The momentum of the bike sent the Biter sprawling. The other Biter was coming towards Neil, bloodied mouth open, ready to bite, when Neil screamed at Neha to steer the bike.

'Mickey Mouse, meet Bunny Ears.'

With that, he swung the metal rod over his head and crushed the Biter's skull in one blow. The older Biter was scrambling to get back up, but by then Neil had sped away down the highway.

For the next ten minutes or so, they rode in relative peace, and with fewer cars visible on the road. Then up ahead Neil saw some vehicles moving at high speed. There were a couple of SUVs and what looked like five large Army trucks. The windows of the lead SUV were rolled down and rifles stuck out at least one window.

'They look like Army vehicles. Maybe they're also heading for the airport.'

Just then, Neil was racked by a violent coughing fit, and he barely managed to bring the bike to a stop before he fell off. Neha had fallen and scraped her knees, but she hardly noticed the pain as she ran towards Neil.

Neil was now on his knees and continuing to cough. The front of his shirt was now coated with blood and his hands were beginning to shake.

Neha started to cry, but Neil got up and pushed her towards the bike.

'Not yet, not yet. I have to get you to safety. I may not last till the airport but I can get you to those Army trucks.'

Neil drove faster than he had ever driven before, with Neha clutching him tightly as he bore down on the vehicles he had seen. He saw someone lift the flap on the rear truck's cab, and a rifle peeked out. Neil wanted to shout at them to not shoot, but when he opened his mouth, more blood came out. He would just have to take his chances. He increased his speed and came alongside the lead SUV, motioning frantically for it to stop. A man in military uniform pointed a rifle at Neil.

'Sir, I will shoot if you do not move away from this convoy.'

Neha shouted back, 'We need help. I'm trying to get to that safe zone at the airport, and my boyfriend needs medical help.'

The man with the rifle turned to talk to someone inside and then another face peered out, a familiar face. Then the convoy came to a halt and a man in an Indian Army uniform ran out from the SUV. He addressed Neha.

'Ma'am, were you with the Make-A-Wish Foundation?'

When Neha nodded, he pointed back to the SUV.

'We really don't have space in there for anyone, but Dr. Gladwell recognized you from the foundation and is asking that we take you along. Anyway, the airport is gone, so we're going to another army shelter nearby, and you had best come along.'

He took Neha's hand and was pulling her when she looked at Neil. 'Can you help him?'

The soldier looked at Neil, pity in his eyes as he took in Neil's bloodied clothes and his yellowing eyes. 'Ma'am, I'm really sorry. We can't do anything for him any more. We need to get going.'

When Neha hesitated, Neil took her hand. 'Please go, Neha, and take care of yourself.'

He was saying the words in his mind, but he realized they were coming out all garbled as more blood came out of his mouth. He felt another sharp stab of pain in his chest and he pushed Neha away. The soldier half dragged her to the SUV and then the convoy drove away.

Neil sat down by the side of the road, watching the vehicles disappear into the distance. He coughed out more blood and then lay down, unable to sit any more. His body felt like it was on fire, but he smiled one last time. He had managed to get Neha to safety, and she had called him her boyfriend, had she not?

With that last thought, Neil George relaxed, closed his eyes and awaited what was to come.

WE'LL NAME HER ALICE

'BOB, I NEED SOME AMERICAN Chopsuey NOW!'
Robert Gladwell put the phone down with
a sigh. He might be the second-in-command
at the American Embassy in New Delhi, but when it came
to his wife, Joanne, there was no question who was in
charge. Especially when she was cranky, sleepless and
in the middle of a very tough pregnancy.

They had been in New Delhi for close to two years,
and Gladwell had been through enough Third World
postings in places like Bangkok, Jakarta and Riyadh to
appreciate the real richness of cultures and relationships
that lay beneath the surface.

He told his secretary that he was going to take a
slightly longer than normal lunch break and as he
told his driver to head to their apartment in the city's
Diplomatic Enclave, he called ahead to order some
Chinese food. He had long realized that the Chinese food
available in India was nothing like what he had tasted
in the US, or indeed during his trips to China when he
had been on a trade delegation. It was spiced, fried and
tossed in ways that were possible only in India, and the
crispy noodles with oversweet sauce ambitiously named

'American Chopsuey' most Americans would have found neither American nor Chopsuey. But who was Gladwell to argue with a pregnant woman's cravings?

'Dan, after lunch, I think I'll stop by for the briefing at South Block.'

Gladwell put down his phone after telling his Personal Security Officer in the car following him about his plans and thought about just how much things had changed. A year ago, security would no doubt have been tight, but he would not be tailed by a contingent of officers from both the US Diplomatic Security Service and India's Special Protection Group, even when he headed out for a quiet family dinner.

The world was imploding fast—tensions in the Middle East had reached a fever pitch, and the attacks on Israeli diplomats in New Delhi in early 2012 had proven to be just a small preview of what was to follow. Attacks on US and Israeli diplomats had occurred through the rest of the year around the world, and the finger of suspicion had always pointed back to Iran. Israel was itching to bomb Iran, and the US efforts at holding it back were fast slipping. Being in India put Gladwell and his team in an especially uncomfortable place. India, while allied to the US, had important commercial interests in Iran, and was also reeling from constant attacks from terrorists based in Pakistan, a nation the US was relying on to allow some sort of orderly withdrawal from the festering mess that was Afghanistan.

Just thinking of it all gave Gladwell a headache, and he was not looking forward to the afternoon's briefing by India's External Affairs Ministry, where they would share intelligence about how rogue Jihadi elements were dangerously close to getting control of Pakistan's nuclear arsenal. Gladwell had seen it all before, in files sent his way by the CIA, but the leadership back in the United States was choosing to stay strangely mum about it all. If all of that was not bad enough, then there was the recent virus in China that had led relations between China and the US to hit rock bottom, and the occasional skirmishes between Chinese and Taiwanese forces did not help. Between Jo's mood swings and the chaos at work, Robert Gladwell looked forward to the pint of beer he had been promised by an old Army buddy who was in town later that evening.

'Hey, Dad, don't tell me Mom wanted that Chopsuey crap again!'

'Young lady, you watch your language.'

Gladwell waited to see the expression on his ten-year old daughter's face gradually change from one of amusement to one of concern. Gladwell rarely lost his temper, but she knew that it wasn't a great idea to make him do so. Finally, he smiled and ruffled her hair.

'Put your school bag in your room and help me set the table, and to make up for the Chopsuey, we'll have some ice cream after lunch.'

Jane whooped and ran more than walked to her room, as Gladwell went to meet his wife, Joanne.

Dr. Joanne Gladwell was six months pregnant and now very much showing it, but she still insisted on participating in the one thing beyond her family that she was passionate about—the Make-A-Wish foundation. She had a Doctorate in Literature and had taught for some years, but gradually found it hard to sustain a teaching career with the constant moves that came with being the wife of a Foreign Service Officer. So she channeled her energy and passion into volunteer work. As Gladwell walked into their bedroom, she was reading up on some of the fundraising plans for the foundation.

'Sweetheart, how're you feeling today?' Gladwell leaned over and kissed her on her forehead, lovingly playing with her blonde hair. Jo held his hand and made him sit down next to her. 'What are you looking at?'

Jo smiled as she answered. 'At my knight in shining armor, my bearer of American Chopsuey.'

Gladwell laughed and got up to set the table.

'Sweetheart, I'll rush through lunch a bit as I have a meeting to get to. By the way, how's the little one?'

Jo grimaced a bit.

'She's kicking, as always. This one will be a real firecracker.'

Jane had been a dream pregnancy and a real angel to bring up. Their second child, a girl, as they had learned in an ultrasound back in the US, was quite the opposite. Jo had terrible morning sickness in the early months, and now, the little one never seemed to stay still.

A rushed lunch later, Gladwell was at the meeting, but it was the press conference in the evening that he dreaded more.

~ * * * ~

'Mr. Gladwell, what can you tell us about what is happening in China and what is your reaction to the Chinese government's accusation that this virus is the result of biological warfare by the United States?'

Gladwell had been wondering when the question

would be asked. The first thirty minutes of the press briefing had been routine questions about the Middle East and the situation in Pakistan, for which Gladwell had stock platitudes ready. But the China situation was one where Gladwell had received no instructions or briefing from his bosses back in Washington. All he knew from intelligence reports was that an unknown virus was raging in China, with the epicenter being a remote military installation in Mongolia. The Chinese had tried to hush it up, a tactic that backfired when the virus exploded after three days. Reports were sketchy, and Gladwell personally thought stories of frenzied victims attacking others were over the top. He wished the Ambassador had been around, but he was on a vacation back in the US, and Gladwell had been left holding the fort.

He took the mike. 'I'm sorry, but I have no information to share on that beyond what Washington has already shared.'

An hour later, Gladwell was seated at a pub with Joshua Abernathy, a face from his past life. As often happened with close friends, there was no need for small talk, even though they were meeting after a dozen years. After hugging each other and ordering drinks, they sipped their beer in silence and only when Gladwell started his second pint did Joshua speak what was on his mind.

'Things are going to get real ugly. You thought of getting your family somewhere safe, with Jo being pregnant and all?'

'Aren't you overreacting? India and Pakistan have been playing these games for years, and even if the shit does hit the fan in the Middle East, we should be safe here.'

Joshua put his mug down and his eyes were creased with worry. 'That's not what I'm talking about. You do remember what I did when I left the Army, don't you?'

Gladwell still didn't know where Joshua was going with this, and motioned to Joshua to wait as he ordered another round of drinks.

'Bob, you need to pay attention, please.'

That got his attention, and Gladwell looked at Joshua, curious as to what had spooked his normally unflappable friend.

'I joined Zeus, a PMC. Private Military Contractor. After Bosnia, when we left the Army, my skills were useless in the civilian world and I wasn't as smart as you were to be able to study and become a diplomat. Zeus contacted me, and for a while it was fun. I ran protection duties for VIPs, hooked up security for international summits and so on, and it paid well. But then it got ugly.'

Gladwell waited as Joshua paused to take a sip, and then continued, an edge to his voice.

'My bosses seemed too well-connected. As I got deeper into the organization, they would regularly meet folks at the State Department and even the White House. Then I was transferred to their Special Division, which, as I quickly learnt, did a bunch of black ops that could be denied by the people ordering them as no US forces would be involved. Stuff like illegal renditions, and hits on targets in countries we'd normally consider friendly.'

Bob could see his friend was worried, but none of this was news. PMCs had mushroomed in the 90s and the War on Terror had provided them a lot of scope to peddle their wares to the highest bidder. Some had grown to have resources to train and equip whole armies for tinpot dictators. But then Joshua continued.

'There are Zeus operatives crawling all over this city. I left Zeus a year ago when I couldn't handle their dirty business any longer, but I still have contacts there. They're all over the Middle East, China and Asia, and it can't be a coincidence that trouble is being stirred up there.'

'Zeus may be powerful but they can't be doing all this on their own. That sounds too far-fetched.'

Joshua leaned over. 'That's what I'm trying to tell you. There are folks in our own system making this happen.'

Joshua's words stayed with Gladwell, but he found it hard to believe that elements in the government could have been engineering this level of chaos. Sure, he was no babe in the woods, and he knew that politicians and business interests were not above dirty tricks to suit their agendas, but something on this scale, with such global ramifications—that did not make any sense.

He spent the evening at home, playing on their PS3 with Jane and then helping Jo decorate the room they had already assigned to their new baby. At night, as had happened for a few weeks, they sat together and debated baby names

'Alexis?'

'No, sounds too strong. I want a nice, feminine name.'

'Lucy?'

'Too common.'

And on it went till they had added a couple of additional names to their already long shortlist.

~ * * * ~

'Bob, this guy's refusing to go away. Sorry to bug you on this but could you help out?'

Gladwell groaned and got up from his desk. He couldn't blame his secretary for asking him to help. This Major Appleseed had been coming to the Embassy for two days, flashing all sorts of credentials, and asking for information that he had no right to ask for. So now Gladwell would have to take on the unpleasant task of turning him away.

For all the pain he was causing, Appleseed was a serving officer in the US Army so Gladwell did him the courtesy of calling him to his office and asking for some coffee to be served. As Appleseed walked in, Gladwell saw that the bull analogy was quite appropriate given Appleseed's bulk. As he began speaking, Gladwell found himself taking an instinctive dislike to him. He was eager and friendly in the manner of a pushy car salesman.

'Morning, Gladwell. Am I glad I got to meet you instead of trying to convince those bureaucrats down there to help me out. This person of interest I'm looking for has registered at the Embassy and I'm hoping you can make my life simple and tell me where she is.'

Gladwell kept his tone pleasant, but his voice had an edge to it. 'Major Appleseed, as others have explained to you already, we cannot share details of where a particular US citizen is staying in Delhi because you have no apparent need to know.'

When Appleseed fished inside his coat pocket for some papers, Gladwell waved them aside. 'You have personal letters from some senators and a supposedly verbal instruction from the Vice President. Unless I have something more formal than that, I am not going to compromise the privacy of a US citizen.'

Appleseed's smile disappeared, to be replaced by a look of disdain. 'Look, Gladwell, I was just trying to save myself time. I can get what I need in a couple of days.' As he began to walk out the door, he turned to look at Gladwell. 'I see your desire to play Boy Scout has not gone away. I've seen your Army files, and if I were you, I would get with the program. The people I work for will need people they can trust, and will have no patience for those who stand in their way.'

Gladwell stood up, barely controlling his anger. 'Major, I have seen *your* files and I can see why you picked up the moniker of the 'Beast of Kandahar'. With the human rights violations you are accused of, you should be in jail. I suppose your political connections are bailing you out, but I have no room for them here. Goodbye.'

As Appleseed slammed the door on the way out, Gladwell sat down, trying to calm down. Appleseed had struck a nerve, one Gladwell had tried to keep buried. As a young officer straight out of training, he had been on a peacekeeping mission in Bosnia, with orders not to intervene unless his men were fired on. They had stumbled upon a group of masked gunmen who had lined up several dozen young men and boys and had begun to execute them. After repeated pleas over the radio to get permission to intervene, he had acted on his conscience and ordered his men to open fire. Eight of the gunmen were killed but instead of being rewarded for saving dozens of civilians, Gladwell found his military career in tatters, especially when it was revealed that the gunmen were on the payroll of a US Private Military Contractor with links to powerful senators. The case was buried and Gladwell was given an honorable discharge. A change in administration gave him the opportunity to rejoin the government but this time as a diplomat, determined to not let such perversities of foreign policy happen again. With people like Appleseed on the loose, and what his friend had mentioned about Zeus operatives, he was not so sure that he or anyone else could come in the way of the sort of evil that Appleseed and his masters represented.

As he headed home, he wondered who Appleseed had been so interested in. He hadn't even bothered to ask his staff, but then it was the principle that mattered. Gladwell closed his eyes and tried to wish away the throbbing headache.

~ * * * ~

'Honey, I'm sorry, but you need to listen to me when I tell you something. You are not going out today. Am I clear?'

Gladwell had shouted much louder than he had intended to, but the accumulated stress of the last two days was beginning to tell on him. Jane sulked and ran sobbing to her room. 'You made me miss my ballet performance in school. You know how much I've prepared for that.'

Gladwell winced as she slammed the door to her room, but he had already vented enough at her to take her to task for this display of defiance. He felt a hand on his shoulder.

'You're beginning to scare me. First you tell me not to step outside of the home, now Jane, and why on Earth do you have a gun in our house? Will you please tell me what's going on?'

Gladwell took his wife's hand in his and slumped against her, finally feeling himself unable to bear all the pressure and tension he had been under for the last two days. He asked Jo to sit down, and she sat down on his lap, trying to calm him down.

'Do you know all the stuff that's on TV about the virus in China and reports about something like it in the US?'

When Jo nodded, he continued, finding that sharing what was plaguing him made it a bit easier to bear, though he was now passing on a terrible burden onto Jo. But if things were going to unravel as fast as he feared, she needed to be prepared.

'The news channels are downplaying it, making it seem like something like bird flu or swine flu. But it's not, it's much, much worse.'

'Do you mean worse in terms of people dying from it?'

Gladwell fumbled for a while, trying to put into words what little he had learned. 'This virus does something to people. It doesn't kill them, but it changes them. They start attacking others. I don't know much more, but I do know they are about to declare martial law in some parts of the US.'

He could tell by the expression on Jo's face just how difficult she found it to believe this. 'I'm sure they'll cure it. It's just a virus...'

Gladwell cut her off. 'Jo, I don't know a lot, but I've

read some cables that show it's spreading faster than anyone thought and its effects are like nothing anyone's seen. Then you have half the planet going to war at the same time, and nobody has a handle on things any more. I heard the first cases in India are being reported so I want you guys to stay home.'

'What happens now?'

Gladwell stood up, gathering his coat. He was now on more familiar ground. While the danger was very real and imminent, he knew the emergency evacuation procedures were in place and his government would not let him and the other Embassy staffers down.

'Don't worry, sweetheart. If the shit does hit the fan, they'll get us out.'

~ * * * ~

'I'm sorry to disturb you personally, Madam Vice President, but nobody seems to be seeing the gravity of the situation. There are cases in India now and the media is still largely ignoring the spread. All I'm asking is that we authorize an emergency evacuation of the families of Embassy staff here. I and a skeleton staff will stay behind.'

Gladwell had sent many cables to Washington making the same request, and many of his colleagues around the world were making similar pleas. What was puzzling was that nobody in Washington seemed to care. It was as if they thought they could wish away the crisis by denying it existed. So Gladwell had taken the risky gambit of going all the way to the top. One of his mentors had been a White House staffer, and while he was unable to help directly, he was able to at least set up this call.

Deborah Henfield's voice boomed over the speakerphone.

'I am Deb Henfield, the Vice President of the United States and I say that there is no imminent crisis based on all the information I have.'

With that, all of Gladwell's worries were dismissed out of hand.

In just one day, things had spiraled horribly out of control. Many large cities in the US were now affected by the virus, and the government had reacted with a media blackout. Bizarrely, the Armed Forces had not been called out to help deal with the crisis, supposedly because they were needed to deal with crises overseas, Zeus had been appointed to deal with containing the unrest and chaos in the US. Regional wars had broken out all over the place and it looked as if the whole world had lost its sanity at the same time.

Gladwell's phone rang. It was Brigadier Randhawa, an Indian Army officer whom he had befriended during his stint in Delhi. The Brigadier was as blunt as ever. 'Bob, our governments don't give a fuck and things will go downhill soon. I have my men ready with our families to get to our base in Manesar. If you want, we'll pick you and your people up.'

Gladwell thanked him and hung up. Randhawa was a highly decorated soldier and was part of the National Security Guard, India's elite commando force, and if there was one place where safety could be found, it was with him and his men.

The next thing he did was to call the head of the Marine detachment at the Embassy. With outbreak cases reported across India, Gladwell had already asked the Marines to be ready for any eventuality.

The Embassy was already full of anxious American citizens, many of them now stranded. Several international flights had already been cancelled as authorities panicked. At first, a few had been outraged at what was happening back in the United States, especially since Zeus mercenaries were in charge of law and order in the US. But now everyone had bigger things to worry about. Rumors that the first cases had been reported in Delhi had sent everyone into a panic and Gladwell was increasingly torn between staying at the Embassy to hold things together or getting home to be with Jo and Jane.

He also saw with increasing irritation that Appleseed was back at the Embassy. As a serving Army Officer, he had every right to be there, but what irked Gladwell was the fact that he was bringing in a gaggle of black-suited men, who were on paper US citizens in Delhi on business trips. Again, going by the book, there was nothing Gladwell could do to stop them, but the fact that their employer was Zeus told Gladwell where Appleseed's true allegiance lay and also made him even more concerned.

'Dr. Dasgupta is here to meet you.'

Gladwell normally would never have entertained a meeting request at a time like this, but this lady had called multiple times and had said that it was a life-and-death situation. He had done background checks on her and he could not figure out what had made her so anxious to meet him. She had recently resigned from some government-funded lab to come back to India.

He finished a couple of emails and then was about to

tell his secretary to send his visitor up when his phone rang. He sat down when he realized the call was from the White House. The President had been largely invisible in the preceding days and the VP had been the public face of the government. Remembering his last conversation with her, Gladwell hoped that she was not too ticked off.

'I am calling you on an urgent national security matter that you need to know. We have been tracking a person of interest called Protima Dasgupta who we believe to have links with terror groups. Do not meet her or allow her access to the Embassy. We have men on the ground who will deal with her.'

Then she hung up, leaving Gladwell flabbergasted. He found it odd that the Vice President would call about a matter like this, but then he also knew that he was hardly privy to all the classified operations sometimes going on under his nose. The last thing he wanted in the middle of all this chaos was a terror suspect loose in his Embassy. He dialed his secretary.

'Tell Dr. Dasgupta that I'm busy and I cannot meet her today.'

When his mobile phone rang, it was Jo, and she sounded terrified.

'Bob, they're calling these things Biters, and I've got calls from friends saying they're right in the middle of Delhi.'

~ * * * ~

'Sir, do we open fire?'

'No, Jim, just get us home. Randhawa asked us to link up with his convoy on the way to National Highway

8, and we don't have much time.'

The SUV sped through the streets of Delhi, and not for the first time, the driver ran over a Biter who got in the way. Under normal circumstances, Gladwell would have been horrified at the thought of running over people in his rush to get home, but things were anything but normal.

In the minutes following Jo's call, all hell seemed to have broken loose. There were rumors that Biters were all over central Delhi, and Gladwell tried one last time to get through to his superiors and ask them to send help, but nobody was picking up the phone. The news was reporting that the President and Vice President had already been evacuated and that the US mainland was now teeming with Biters. Then came the news that tactical nuclear attacks had been launched on Indian Army targets by Pakistan, and that India was in the process of retaliating.

Gladwell took an hour to ensure that the staffers got transport home, in many cases relying on the Marines to stop taxis for them. He wished there was more he could do for the US citizens at the Embassy, but after talking to Randhawa, he was told that there were only five trucks, and there was no room for others. Gladwell had agreed on a rendezvous point with Randhawa and asked all his staffers to get there with their families. He only hoped most of them would get there safely.

Gladwell had initially been skeptical about the rumors about the Biters being bloodthirsty monsters who could not be killed. But in the ten minutes since they had left the Embassy, he was more scared than he had ever been before. All around him, small groups of Biters, covered in blood and grotesque wounds, roamed through the city at will, attacking anyone they saw. He saw a couple of police posts that had been overrun, and his stomach had churned at the sight of what had remained of the policemen.

The SUV screeched to a halt outside Gladwell's home and the two Marines at the back stepped out, their assault rifles at the ready. The driver was also armed, but he kept the engine running as Gladwell sprinted inside and came out a minute later with Jo and Jane. As he herded them into the vehicle, Jane saw a trio of Biters walk towards them and she screamed. That got their attention and they increased their pace.

'Get inside now!'

Jane was now crying in terror and had to be bodily lifted inside the vehicle. The driver backed away and began the journey to the highway where they were to link up with Randhawa. In theory it was only a twenty-minute drive, but now they were going to drive through a city teeming with Biters.

~ * * * ~

'Sir, the road's too blocked with cars. There's no way we can proceed!'

Between the driver's increasingly panic-stricken updates, Jane's continuous sobbing and one of the Marines' loud prayers, Gladwell was having trouble concentrating on keeping all of them alive. This was the third dead end they had hit in the last ten minutes, and he was beginning to regret having taken the SUV in the first place. True, they comfortably fit into it, but with the streets littered with abandoned vehicles, it was that much tougher to find a way through the maze. On the flip side, they had managed to store some stocks of drinking water and canned food in the trunk, but Gladwell was pretty sure by now that they were at more imminent risk of dying at the hands of Biters instead of thirst or hunger.

The first time he had seen one of the Biters' victims get up and join in the rampage, his heart had nearly stopped. He had turned around to see if he could somehow shield Jane, but he found her watching with tear-filled eyes. He did not know if he could protect her physically, but he knew he had already failed to shield her from the horror unfolding all around them.

There were bodies strewn around this stretch of the road, as a company of troops, who had rushed into action without knowing what they were up against, had been torn apart. Gladwell had noticed a couple of things so far—one, that the Biters massacred anyone who tried to resist, and second, that for all their terrifying invulnerability to bullets, they could be killed. Two Biters lying in pools of blood near the scene of this battle told him that. But for now, he could not contemplate what that weakness must be, since there were at least a dozen Biters bearing down on them.

'Back off, we'll find another side street!'

Gladwell was trying to sound confident, but he knew that they were lost. In trying to get around the maze of cars and trying to avoid large groups of Biters, they had strayed too far from the main roads, and were now trying to find their way through a warren of smaller side streets. The two Marines had their rifles ready, but there was no way they were going to roll down the windows. By now Jane had pretty much cried herself into silence, and truth be told, the one who had most kept her wits about her was Jo. She had her left hand on her belly, saying soothing things to their unborn daughter, and in her right hand was a map of Delhi, with which she was now trying to guide them. She caught Gladwell looking at her and he just smiled and patted her knee. He wanted to tell her how proud he was of her strength and how looking at her was making him feel braver than he really was, but for now that little gesture said more than he could have hoped to have said in many minutes.

'Go straight and then turn right at the next traffic light. We should get onto a major road and then you can find your way to the highway.'

'Yes, Ma'am.'

The SUV careened down the narrow street and for a moment Gladwell thought that they had finally got a lucky break. The street seemed to be abandoned. That was when the four Biters ran into their path.

If the driver had maintained his speed, he could have run over the lead Biter, but he panicked and swerved the SUV hard to the left. They hit one Biter and flung him to the side but brought the SUV to a halt. As he fumbled with the keys to start the engine again, the other three Biters started banging on the windows.

This was the closest Gladwell had come to a Biter so far and he looked at the bloodied face staring at him from just a few inches away, separated only by the glass of the window. The man was wearing what had once been perhaps an expensive pair of designer sunglasses, but now the shattered remains of those hung from one ear.

His eyes were vacant and drool and blood were streaming down his mouth. He had been bitten several times on his neck and shoulder, and blood from those wounds joined that from his mouth to almost completely cover the front of his shirt. He was banging on the window with both hands and, not able to make much headway, he began banging his head against it.

Gladwell was carrying his gun, a small .25 Guernica he had acquired a license for a few months ago after the attacks on diplomats intensified. The glass cracked as the Biter kept banging his head against it, and without thinking, Gladwell raised his gun and fired a single round straight into the Biter's forehead. The Biter rocked back and fell onto the pavement, and as blood seeped out of the single hole in the middle of his head, he did not show any signs of getting up. Gladwell screamed to the Marines in the rearmost seats.

'Shoot them in the head! Aim for their heads!'

Galvanized into action by Gladwell's words, the Marines selected single-shot mode on their M-16s and fired a single round each into the heads of the Biters attacking the rear windows. Both Biters went down and did not get back up. By now, the driver had recovered enough of his wits and started the SUV again.

Everyone sat in silence, watching the alleys around them for any further signs of Biters. Gladwell gripped his pistol in both hands, scanning both sides of the road. He knew that they still had a long way to go, but at least they had learned one important lesson—Biters could be defeated.

~ * * * ~

'I can see three more cars!'

The cry from Jo got everyone's attention. They had proceeded relatively unmolested for the last fifteen minutes and were now close to the rendezvous point agreed with Randhawa. This was at the point where the road intersected with the National Highway, and Gladwell was heartened to see three cars already there. His spirits rose at the thought that the staffers and their families had made it. There was no sign of Randhawa, but then Gladwell expected that they would make slower progress in their trucks. One of the Marines opened the door as the SUV stopped and was about to step out when Gladwell stopped him.

'Not so fast. Something doesn't seem right.'

He recognized at least one of the cars as belonging to his staffers, but there was no sign of anyone there, and a couple of the cars had their doors open. He asked the driver to keep the engine running and stepped out, followed by one of the Marines. The other Marine stayed in the vehicle to provide some cover for Jo and Jane in case there was any trouble.

Gladwell had his gun in his hand, and try as he might, he could not stop his hand shaking. He had seen combat up close in the Balkans, but that was many years ago, and he had been facing men, ruthless mercenaries but men like himself, who would bleed and die, not ghouls of the sort that now roamed through Delhi. Something moved behind one of the cars and he readied his gun, holding it in both hands, both to steady his aim and stop his hands shaking. He motioned to the Marine to give him cover and then he peered around the car. He was in no way prepared for what he saw.

It was, or rather had been, Jonathan, a young staffer at the Embassy who had been there for less than a year. His blond hair was matted with blood and his lean, dimpled face that had once set many a woman's heart aflutter at Embassy parties was pulled back in a grotesque grimace. His eyes were closed and his breath came in ragged gasps. The front of his shirt was covered in blood. As Gladwell leaned closer to see if he was okay, his eyes snapped open, and instinctively Gladwell took a step back.

Jonathan's lively blue eyes were gone, replaced by a yellowed stare that Gladwell had seen earlier in the Biters that had attacked their SUV. Jonathan's mouth opened, and for a second Gladwell hoped that he might say something, that his humanity might yet be preserved. Instead, he emitted a low growl that was more animal than human. He bared his teeth and snapped at Gladwell, who jumped back. Gladwell's gun was pointed at the figure in front of him, but Gladwell could not bring himself to shoot someone who had till a few hours ago been a friend.

He stumbled back towards the SUV, almost bumping into the Marine, whose eyes widened as he saw the figure shuffling towards them. He had his M-16 raised, but Gladwell could tell by the hesitation in his eyes that he was also having trouble pulling the trigger.

A group emerged from the side of the road. There were two more staffers, their wives and, most horrifying of all, their four children. They shuffled towards Gladwell, teeth bared, their clothes and bodies covered in blood, and Gladwell gave up all pretense of bravado.

'Run!'

The two of them sprinted to the SUV and he could tell by Jane's haunted expression that she had seen everything. He got into the front seat and asked the driver to pass the cars and get on the highway. He called Randhawa. He heard the soldier's voice on the third ring, but had to strain to hear what Randhawa was saying as every word seemed to be cut off by loud pops.

'We're fighting our way through an absolute mob of Biters. Get on the highway and wait for us. We'll catch up soon enough.'

~ * * * ~

'Sir, we can't just wait here in the middle of the highway. We'll be a magnet for Biters for miles around.'

Gladwell knew that there was a lot of truth in what the Marine had said. But the people gathered around him were waiting for him to make a decision. It was one thing to decide on matters of protocol sitting in his air-conditioned office, quite another to be making life-and-death decisions in the middle of a warzone.

Waiting for Randhawa and his men left them exposed since Randhawa was at least twenty minutes away and his last conversation had been interrupted several times by the sound of automatic fire. On the other hand, their chances of survival on their own were slim. He did not know the exact location of the base they were headed towards and even if he got that from Randhawa, he did not fancy his chances of getting there in one car with four armed men. The outlying areas of Delhi they would have to pass were slums. Once the contagion had taken hold, it had taken mere hours to spread through those packed shanty huts. The local radio channels had stopped broadcasting an hour ago but the Internet still seemed to be up and Jo had read out heartwrenching updates on thousands of Biters from these slums spilling over into posh condominiums built in the suburbs. The impoverished and the elite had become one as a bloodthirsty mob of Biters that was consuming everyone in its path and fast spreading towards the city center.

'We wait.'

Gladwell stared down the young Marine till it was clear who was in charge. Then he got to work, half-forgotten training and half-remembered instincts taking over. For a second, he was brought back to a misty morning in Bosnia.

Then, as now, he was a reluctant warrior forced to fight to save innocent lives. There were two big differences. One, he was no longer a twenty-two-year-old who believed he could not be touched, and second, he was now fighting for his family. The first made him less impulsive and the second made him determined that if the Biters got to Jo or Jane, they would do so by stepping over his corpse.

He asked for the SUV to be parked near the side of the road on the large flyover. That ensured they could not be attacked from behind and also that they would have the advantage of height. Neither of the Marines had seen combat before and Gladwell gave them sentry duty, hoping that they would be too busy to be afraid. The driver was a Diplomatic Service agent who had served in the Middle East and quickly got the Marines in place.

Gladwell felt a hand on his arm. It was Jo. 'Bob, ask the Marines to give me and Jane their handguns and tell us how to shoot them if we need to.'

Gladwell didn't know what to say. His family was in as much danger as the rest of them but he had never contemplated little Jane and his own Jo carrying guns.

Jim, the driver, cut in. 'Sir, she's right. If there are as many Biters out there as they say, we'll need every gun we can get.'

And so they began the wait for Randhawa and his men, watching the roads and slums nearby for Biters.

They did not have to wait long. Their position overlooked the Radisson hotel, and one of the Marines shouted out a warning that he had spotted some movement. Looking down from their vantage point, they saw the first of the Biters appear from among the decrepit shops that surrounded the area and then several more appeared from the shattered front door of the Radisson. As Gladwell watched, their numbers continued to swell till many hundreds of Biters streamed out of the buildings, heading towards the city. Gladwell's first thought was that they seemed to be like a swarm of locusts, consuming everything in their path, but he knew they were much more dangerous, for with each victim they swelled their ranks till they were too numerous to stop or fight. He looked around him and realized that with their modest numbers and firepower, they would not have lasted more than a few minutes if that mob of Biters had been headed for them.

Deciding quickly that discretion was the better part of valor, he asked everyone to get down, and they all sat with their backs pressed to the side of the road, hearing the thumps and growls of the Biters as they passed under them. Gladwell had put down his gun and was

127

holding Jo's hand with one hand and Jane's with the other. He had never been a particularly religious person, but this seemed like as good a time as any to send up a prayer for the safety of his wife, his daughter and their unborn child.

~ * * * ~

They had been waiting for about ten minutes when Jo whispered, 'Some of them are on the highway.'

Gladwell didn't know if they had been spotted, but a group of about twenty Biters had detached itself and turned onto the flyover where Gladwell's group was huddled. With the SUV partially obscuring them, Gladwell wasn't sure they had been spotted yet, but if the Biters got much closer then there would be no option left but to try and fight it out. Gladwell looked to Jim, aware that of all of them, he had perhaps the most field experience.

'Jim, what do you reckon are our chances of taking them out before they get too close?'

Jim's face bore a grim expression as he answered.

'Not too good, Sir. If those were twenty humans, even trained soldiers, we could have ambushed them now and taken out half of them in the first salvo before they got a shot off. But we need headshots, and they're about two hundred meters out. At that range, we can forget scoring head shots with our handguns, and the two boys with the M-16s aren't exactly trained snipers either.'

'Then we hide as long as we can.'

They huddled against the SUV with Jim lying flat on the ground behind a tire, watching the Biters as they approached. All of them were trying to be as still and as quiet as they could, and then Jane brought her hands up to her nose, trying to stifle a sneeze. Everyone looked at her in dread, the two seconds seeming like an eternity. As the moment passed, they all spontaneously broke out into smiles. And then it happened.

Jane sneezed.

The Biters stopped, looking right and left, and then Gladwell's heart stopped. One of them looked straight at the SUV and roared, and they began shuffling towards the SUV as fast as they could.

'Marines, fire at will!'

Gladwell's roared command galvanized the two Marines into action and they stepped out from behind the SUV, their M-16s at the ready.

'Single shot only. Aim for the head. Only the head.'

As the Marines took aim and began firing at the approaching group of Biters, Gladwell and the others took aim with their handguns. Gladwell ensured the safety was off on Jane and Jo's guns and steadied Jane's hands, pointing them towards the Biters.

'Sweetheart, don't worry about the heads. At this range, we won't hit them with pistols. Aim for the legs so we can at least slow them down. Take a deep breath, count to three, aim and fire, and then repeat. Don't fire blindly or too fast.'

And then the group opened fire in a deadly volley that would have massacred any human opponents. With the Biters, it had less of a dramatic effect. The two Marines were trying their best, but with the Biters moving, most of their initial shots missed their targets. Some hit the Biters in the chest and neck, and sent them staggering back till they resumed their approach. Then one of them scored a direct headshot and the Biter went down for good. The group cheered, but it was a small victory.

That still left almost twenty Biters now closing in on them. Jane and Jo were firing away and Gladwell noted with dismay that most of their bullets were pinging off the pavement around the Biters. With human adversaries, even such near misses would have sent them scampering for cover, but Biters did not seem to care. He was about to say something when he saw how badly Jane's hands were shaking.

He took aim, focusing on a large Biter closest to them, a man wearing only a pair of shorts, his bare torso covered in blood and gore. Gladwell fired two rounds, one smacking into the Biter's thigh, the second hitting him in the stomach. The Biter doubled over for a second and then straightened up and made straight for him. Jim and the Marines had been busy and at least three Biters were down but now they were less than fifty meters away and it was a matter of time before the Biters overwhelmed them.

That was when Gladwell did something quite extraordinary. Under normal circumstances Gladwell would never have worked up the insane courage to do something like this, but all Gladwell could think of was protecting his family and so he stepped into the middle of the highway and began to walk briskly towards the Biters. Jo screamed out his name and he did not look back as he replied.

'Keep shooting!'

He was now less than ten feet away from the nearest Biter, a thin man wearing a bloodied Superman t-shirt.

Gladwell shouted back, though he would have no recollection of what he had said, though much later Jo claimed he had said something along the lines of 'Eat shit and die'. Gladwell felt a stab of fear as the Biter came closer, and he tried to give him a name, to think he was a living, breathing enemy who could be killed, not some undead monster. So this one naturally became Superman.

As Superman howled, Gladwell put a bullet through his forehead, sending him flopping down on the road. Gladwell was hardly a crack shot, but at such close range, he did not need to try too hard. Another Biter, this one a woman with flowing long hair now matted with blood oozing from her neck, took his place and came towards him. Gladwell missed with his first shot, which hit her in the shoulder, but the second put Rapunzel down for good. Another Biter went down from a headshot, and he turned to see that Jim had joined him. The two Marines had also come to join them and at such close quarters, they were putting down Biters with almost every shot. A large Biter, who towered over him, came so close that Gladwell could smell his putrid breath and see the yellow gore on the corners of his mouth. He put a bullet in his mouth and as the Biter staggered back, Gladwell kicked him in the gut and shot him in the head.

Gladwell was suddenly aware that the Biters were no longer just in front of him but beside him. In the chaos of the battle, he was no longer facing a mob of Biters but in the middle of one. He shot another Biter down and took a step back as two more Biters reached out towards him.

That was when both Biters fell, their heads cracked

open by direct hits from large-caliber weapons. The deep rumble of heavy engines rose and Gladwell looked up to see several trucks and one SUV. Men in the black commando fatigues of the National Security Guard jumped out of the trucks and began mowing down the Biters with precisely aimed shots to the head. The bearded and turbaned face of Randhawa peered out from the passenger side window of the SUV.

'Gladwell, I thought you were a diplomat but you would put bloody John Rambo to shame. Come on!'

As Gladwell shepherded Jo and Jane into Randhawa's SUV, he turned to see the two Marines and Jim looking at him with an expression he had not seen before. Till now, he had been the ranking diplomat. Now, he was respected. In the new world that faced them all, this was one of the subtle changes they would all come to adapt to—the ranks and badges of the past meant nothing. Respect, and indeed survival, had to be earned in blood.

~ * * * ~

They sat in silence for a few minutes, each of them quietly taking in how everything had changed. Gladwell was glad to see that a few stragglers from the Embassy who had arrived late had been picked up by Randhawa's convoy. In all, they numbered about a hundred men, women and children, all headed towards the relative safety of Randhawa's base.

Jo and Jane were in the back of the SUV with Randhawa's wife and child and four armed commandos, and Randhawa had decided to drive the SUV himself, asking the driver to take a break in the back of one of the trucks. The terrified young soldier had saluted gratefully and jogged back to one of the accompanying trucks.

Unable to contain his curiosity any longer, Gladwell asked Randhawa if he knew any more about what was happening in the world. Randhawa looked at him with bloodshot eyes. 'It's really the bloody end of the world, that's what it is. First we have these Biters crawling out of every frigging corner, and what they haven't ripped apart, we will ourselves.'

When Gladwell asked what he meant, he got a chilling account of the multiple nuclear battles being waged. Contact with much of the Middle East had been lost as Iran and Israel engaged in a last orgy of mutual nuclear annihilation that engulfed much of the region. Chinese missiles were flying into Taiwan and India and Pakistan were at each other's throats. Gladwell closed his eyes and sat back, wondering if this was all a bad dream, if he would wake up and find that his biggest worry was fetching American Chopsuey for Jo at odd hours. He opened his eyes, and seeing the abandoned vehicles littering the highway, he realized that the world he had come to take for granted had indeed died. What would arise in its place was a terrifying prospect and he wondered how long he could keep his family safe.

Thunder rumbled and Randhawa flinched before recovering. Randhawa grinned at him, and not for the first time, Gladwell wondered how he could manage to smile at a time like this. 'Never a better time to get out of the city.'

Gladwell looked back and saw smoke rising in the distance from numerous fires that had broken out. He shook his head sadly. Even when human civilization was threatened, man's baser instincts could not be tamed. The soldiers in the back were talking about how they had seen looters rampaging through the streets and with no apparent law and order, raping and pillaging at will. While Randhawa's convoy had fought its way through a large mob of Biters, they had gunned down an equal number of human looters who were rampaging through nearby shops. Someone spoke out on the radio.

'Sir, I see a bike approaching us at high speed.'

'Who's driving it? Are they armed?'

Gladwell could sense the hesitation in the man's voice as he answered Randhawa.

'Sir, there's a young woman in the back, and it's being driven by a kid wearing... rabbit ears of some sort.'

Randhawa slammed his fist on the steering wheel.

'Just what we need. Some drunk kid out on a joyride wearing silly ears. If they come closer, tell them to back off.'

As the bike moved towards them, Gladwell's hand tightened around his gun. The boy's shirt was covered in blood and his face had a desperate look that Gladwell didn't like. One of the soldiers in the back pointed his rifle at the boy.

'Sir, I will shoot if you do not move away from this convoy.'

The girl sitting behind the strange boy with bunny ears raised one of her hands and pleaded.

'We need help. I'm trying to get to that safe zone at the airport, and my boyfriend needs medical help.'

Jo murmured behind him, 'Oh my God, could that be Neha from the foundation?' Jo pushed down the rifle the soldier had pointed at the bike and pleaded with

Randhawa to stop. 'Please, please stop. I think I know that girl from the Make-A-Wish Foundation. We can't just leave them here.'

They were tight on space and Randhawa seemed to be mulling the question over in his mind. Finally, he barked into the radio. 'Stop, everyone stop. One of you in the back go and check who they are.'

One of the soldiers disembarked and went over to the bike, which had stopped alongside the SUV. He talked to the girl, and started to lead her back to the SUV. The girl was sobbing and pointing to the boy, whose eyes had started yellowing. Now that they had stopped, Gladwell and the others got a closer look at him. There was no question about it—he was transforming into a Biter, yet he had somehow got this girl to safety, knowing he was doomed. Gladwell felt a lump in his throat. In the middle of all the madness and hatred, this simple act of sacrifice reminded all of them that being human was still worth clinging on to, still worth fighting for, still something to be proud of. Gladwell thought he saw Randhawa's eyes moisten as well, but the grizzled soldier blinked it away, though he did give a curt nod of respect to the boy. The girl was still sobbing uncontrollably as Jo took her in her arms and then the convoy sped on towards its destination.

~ * * * ~

Gladwell was surprised, though perhaps he should not have been, that the first predators they had to fight off were human.

With the outbreak came a lawlessness that nobody

had ever planned for. Initially there was some looting, but soon people realized that money was of little value any more. Prison doors lay open. Serial killers, sociopaths, rapists—the worst of man came out to wreak their havoc.

Three days into their stay in the base, Gladwell and Randhawa had started seeing small groups of civilians escaping from the madness in the city. They had taken them in, though soon enough supplies and food would be a real issue. Then came those who came not to take refuge, but to prey upon a well-stocked settlement. A settlement with food, supplies and women.

The first attack had been smashed before it had really unfolded. Ten men armed with swords and cleavers had tried to enter the complex at night. The American Marines and Indian commandos, by now trained to aim for the head after all their battles with the Biters, had mistaken the intruders for Biters and felled four with headshots before the others screamed in terror and ran away into the night. The next attack had been more serious, with two jeeps full of armed men, members of a paramilitary unit that had decided to use their weapons and training to their advantage. The firefight had lasted more than thirty minutes before they were driven off. But after that, attacks by looters ceased. Word had spread that this particular settlement was occupied by people not to be messed with easily. In the second attack, Randhawa had been seriously wounded, and by consensus, Gladwell was appointed the leader of their small settlement.

That night, Gladwell sat down next to Jo, who was singing to her unborn daughter, hoping that innocent rhymes would register with her instead of the gunfire and screams that she heard all day.

'How are you doing?'

'She seems to like the noise. She's been kicking all day.'

Gladwell kissed her lightly on the head and then sat down to take stock of their situation. They had plenty of ammunition, but at the rate at which they were attracting new members, they would have to organize some sort of effort to get food. By now, nobody believed that things would get back to normal. Gladwell had organized small patrols to scour the neighboring areas, and they all spoke about Biters running rampant. The Internet was down, and there was nothing on TV, but they did manage to pick up radio transmissions from military channels and from private radio operators.

The picture they painted was terrifying. Most of the world had been laid waste by the wars that had erupted, and by the Biters. There were reports that many governments had authorized nuclear airbursts over major cities in a last-ditch, desperate attempt to wipe out the Biters and reclaim the cities. Gladwell shuddered as he considered what would be happening to the human survivors left in the cities.

The ground shook and he wondered whether on top of all the other catastrophes they had endured, an earthquake was next. That was when Jo screamed out to him. He rushed to her, and Jane came into the small room that they shared with three other families.

A mushroom cloud billowed over the city of Delhi. There had been air strikes on the city for the last couple of days and Gladwell had assumed it was another one but the cloud told him that Delhi had joined the list of cities that had succumbed to this madness.

One of the soldiers had told him that if governments were indeed using air burst nuclear weapons then the risk of residual radiation was small. Moreover, they were almost fifty kilometers away from the city center. That was little consolation to Gladwell as he held his family tight and watched another mushroom cloud join the first one. When they stepped out of the room, all the people in their group were standing there, tears in their eyes. If any of them had still hoped that they might go back home, there was no question of that now.

Gladwell heard someone mumble next to him, 'We killed the world. It's all dead land out here now.'

That evening, their settlement was eerily quiet. Randhawa was still unconscious and Gladwell realized that no matter how low people felt, Biters and human predators would not stop coming. So he spent several hours making a schedule of who would be on guard duty and also scheduling firearms classes for everyone. In the new reality they faced, they would need every single one of them to be able to fight if needed.

Mentally and physically drained, he joined Jo at night. As he walked in, Neha, the young girl they had picked up on the highway, left.

'How's she holding up?'

Jo looked tired and miserable but managed to smile.

'Poor girl's been through a lot. Lost her family and then the young man who got her to us. At least we still have each other.'

Gladwell hugged Jo and sat next to her on the floor. He was due for sentry duty in two hours' time, so he wanted to get as much rest as he could. He ran his hand gently over Jo's stomach.

'How's the little one doing?'

'Still kicking and jumping around.'

'Thought of a name?'

Truth be told, Gladwell was so drained that he no longer had the energy to debate names. He was happy to go with whatever Jo chose.

Jo thought of the bunny-eared young man who had got Neha to safety despite knowing that he was doomed and of the wish they had set out to fulfill. She had heard people start referring to the world outside as Deadland and the name had stuck. While she did not want her daughter to be born into such a world, she was not yet ready to give her hope. So she thought of a name that would pay homage to the brave man wearing bunny ears, a name that harked back to childhood tales of a more innocent time, a name that would hold out the promise of a land filled with wonder, not death.

She looked at Gladwell, her mind made up.

'We'll name her Alice.'

THE END

THE ALICE IN DEADLAND TRILOGY

ALICE IN DEADLAND

C IVILIZATION AS WE KNOW IT ended more than fifteen years ago, leaving as it's legacy barren wastelands called the Deadland and a new terror for the humans who survived—hordes of undead Biters.

Fifteen year-old Alice has spent her entire life in the Deadland, her education consisting of how best to use guns and knives in the ongoing war for survival against the Biters. One day, Alice spots a Biter disappearing into a hole in the ground and follows it, in search of fabled underground Biter bases.

What Alice discovers there propels her into an action-packed adventure that changes her life and that of all humans in the Deadland forever. An adventure where she learns the terrible conspiracy behind the ruin of humanity, the truth behind the origin of the Biters, and the prophecy the mysterious Biter Queen believes Alice is destined to fulfill.

A prophecy based on the charred remains of the last book in the Deadland—a book called Alice in Wonderland.

THROUGH THE LOOKING GLASS

ALICE IN DEADLAND BOOK II

ORE THAN TWO YEARS HAVE passed since Alice followed a Biter with bunny ears down a hole, triggering events that forever changed her life and that of everyone in the Deadland. The Red Guards have been fought to a standstill; Alice has restored some measure of peace between humans and Biters; and under Alice, humans have laid the foundations of the first large, organized community since The Rising—a city called Wonderland.

That peace is shattered in a series of vicious Biter attacks and Alice finds herself shunned by the very people she helped liberate. Now she must re-enter the Deadland to unravel this new conspiracy that threatens Wonderland. Doing so will mean coming face to face with her most deadly adversary ever—the Red Queen..

ABOUT MAINAK DHAR

MAINAK DHAR IS A CUBICLE dweller by day and writer by night, with thirteen books to his credit. He has been published widely by major publishers in India like Random House and Penguin, but took the plunge into self-publishing with the Amazon Kindle Store in March 2011 to reach readers worldwide. In his first year on the Kindle store, he sold more than 100,000 ebooks, making him one of the top selling self-published writers worldwide. He is the author of the Amazon.com bestseller Alice in Deadland and you can learn more about him and his writing at www.mainakdhar.com.

Made in the USA
Lexington, KY
12 December 2012